P9-DXL-338

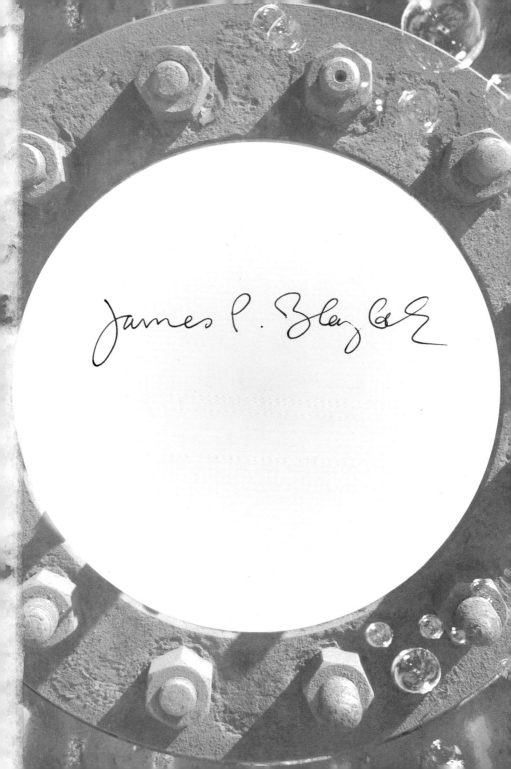

James P. Blaylock

The Ebb Tide:
A Langdon St. Ives
Adventure

The Ebb Tide:
A Langdon St. Ives
Adventure

James P. Blaylock

Illustrated by J. K. Potter

Subterranean Press 2009

uc
8/2012

The Ebb Tide: A Langdon St. Ives Adventure
Copyright © 2009 by James P. Blaylock. All rights reserved.

First Edition

ISBN
978-1-59606-228-3

Subterranean Press
PO Box 190106
Burton, MI 48519

www.subterraneanpress.com

The Ebb Tide

Chapter 1

Merton's Rarities

W E WERE AT THE Half Toad one evè-
ning early in the month of a windy May—
Langdon St. Ives; Tubby Frobisher, and
myself, Jack Owlesby—taking our ease at our customary
table. Professor St. Ives, as you're perhaps already aware,
is one of England's most brilliant scientists, and her most
intrepid explorer. The Half Toad is an inn that lies in
Lambert Court, off Fingal Street in London, frequented
by men of science down on their luck: three rooms to
let, William and Henrietta Billson proprietors. The inn
is difficult to find if you don't know the turning or if you
fail to see the upper body of what is commonly called
a Surinam toad leaning out of the high window over
the door.

The carving of the toad was carried out of Guiana in the mid-century by Billson himself, aboard the old *William Rodgers*. The nether half of the creature blew to flinders when the powder magazine exploded in the dead of night, sinking the ship and half the crew in a fog off Santo Domingo. Billson found himself afloat and alone with half the toad, and he clung to the remains for close onto a day and a half before fishermen hauled him out nearly drowned. He went straight back to London on a mail packet, only to discover that his old father had died two months earlier and left him something over five hundred a year, and so he counted his many blessings, married his sweetheart, and set up shop in Lambert Court, where he put the heroic toad in the window.

In his seagoing days, Billson had been an amateur naturalist, and had sailed as a young man with Sir Gilbert Blane, popularly known as Lemon Juice Blane, the great anti-scorbutic doctor. Billson's collection of fish and amphibiana was housed in the back of the inn (and still is). It was the man's deep interest in Japanese carp that led to his correspondence with St. Ives in the days following the incident of the break-in at the Bayswater Street Oceanarium in the time of the Homunculus.

St. Ives had recently resolved to keep a room the year round at the Half Toad, despite—or rather because of—its obscure location, so that he had secure digs when he came in from Chingford-by-the-Tower to London proper, which happened often enough. Billson wasn't a man to be trifled with, nor a man to ask questions, both of which attributes suited St. Ives down to the ground. Henrietta Billson, a ruddy-faced, smiling woman, once beat a customer half silly with a potato masher who had put his hands on the girl who makes up the rooms. Her fruit tarts and meat pies would make you weep.

Enough people frequent the Inn to keep Billson busy in front of his fireplace spit long into the evening, and on the night in question he had a joint of beef rotating, done very nearly to a turn, and he was looking at it with a practiced eye, his carving knife ready at hand. Beneath, to catch the drippings, hung a kettle of those small potatoes called Irish apricots by the Welsh, and there wasn't a man among us who didn't have the look of a greedy dog.

This particular May evening at the Half Toad, I'll point out in passing, took place during that lamented period when St. Ives had been forbidden entrance to the Explorer's Club because of a minor kitchen mishap involving refined brandy and the head and tentacles of a giant squid. The great man's temporary banishment and subsequent reinstatement will have to be the subject of another account, but in those dark days St. Ives came to appreciate the homely luxury of the Half Toad, and in the years following his reinstatement he visited the

Explorers Club but rarely. I should say "we," since I was (and am) St. Ives's frequent companion when the great man comes into London.

But as I was saying, I remember that May evening in '82 well enough, for the Phoenix Park murders were being shouted high and low by newsboys out on Fingal Street. That unforgettable joint of beef was turning on the spit, there were kidney pies baking in the oven and puddings boiling in the copper, and, of course, there were those potatoes. The Billsons' halfwit kitchen help, a Swede of indeterminate age named Lars Hopeful, was drawing ale from the tap, and all of us, you can be sure, were looking forward to making a long night of it.

I hadn't so much as put the glass to my lips when the door swung open, the street noise momentarily heightened, and we looked up to see who it was coming in with the wind. Surprisingly, it was St. Ives's man Hasbro, who should have been in Chingford tending the home fires, so to speak, and collecting the post. Alice—Mrs. St. Ives—was in Scarborough with the St. Ives children, little Eddie and his sister Cleo. My own wife, Dorothy, had gone along, the lot of them staying with Alice's ancient grandmother, which explains how St. Ives and I had come to be temporarily bachelorized. Hasbro had the air of a man in a hurry (not his usual demeanor) and you can imagine that we were suddenly anxious to hear him out.

Without a word, however, he produced from his coat a recent copy of Merton's *Catalogue of Rarities* and opened it to a folded page, which he passed across to St. Ives, who read the piece aloud. There was offered for sale a hand-drawn map of a small area of the Morecambe Sands, the location not identified. The map, according to the catalogue copy, was stained with waterweeds, tobacco, and salt rime, was torn, soiled, and ill-drawn as if by a child, was signed with the letter K and the crude, figure-eight drawing of a cuttlefish, and was offered for sale for two pounds six. "Of questionable value," Merton had added, "but perhaps interesting to the right party."

Merton had found the right party, and had doubt-less *expected* to find it, because he had sent the catalogue out to St. Ives Manor by messenger, not suspecting, of course, that the Professor was already in London. St. Ives stood up abruptly from his chair and uttered the words, "Kraken's map, or I'm a fried whiting." He slid the catalogue into his coat and along with the waiting Hasbro strode toward the door, shouting a hasty good-bye to Billson, who gestured his farewell with the carving knife. Never a potato did I eat, I'm sad to say, and the same for Tubby Frobisher, who was fast on my heels, although the man could have had no idea what any of this meant.

Night was falling, and the temperature with it, as if the world had tilted and spring had slid back into

winter. Lambert court was deserted aside from a workman in dungarees, who was inordinately tall and sneery,
lounging on a pile of excavated dirt and rock with
the air of a man having avoided a day's work. Twenty
minutes earlier there had been two of them, the other
squat and with dangling, heavy arms, and the comical
contrast between the two had stayed in my mind. Now
the tall one was smoking a pipe over the remains of the
day—Balkan Sobranie, my own tobacco of choice, and
perhaps a little elevated for a workman's pocketbook,
something I remarked to Frobisher when the wind blew
the reek past us in a cloud. The man gathered himself
together and left just as we came out through the door.
He disappeared back through the Court with a certain
celerity, as if he had an appointment to keep.

Fingal Street, never particularly active, was possessed
of an evening quiet. St. Ives hailed a Hansom cab that
happened to be passing, and he and Hasbro climbed
aboard and whirled away. "To Merton's!" St. Ives shouted
back at us, and Tubby and I were left to follow as best we
could. We set out on foot, making our way down toward
the Embankment at a fair pace.

"Look here, Jackie," Frobisher said, puffing along
beside me. "What on Earth is this business of the map?
That was my kidney pie just coming out of the oven, and
now I'm left to starve."

"I can't be certain," I said. "I can only speculate."

"Then speculate me this: a map to *what?* Gold and jewels, eh? Something of that sort? The problem with all this," he told me, "is that anything lost in the Morecambe Sands will stay lost. I've heard stories of coaches and four sinking into the quicksands of Morecambe Bay with all hands on board, never to be seen again. A man might as well have a map of the Bottomless Pit."

"Merton surely knows that," I said. "His 'of doubtful value' makes just that point. Do you remember poor old Bill Kraken?"

"Absolutely. Not a bad sort, although half the time off his chump, as I recall."

"Not so far off as it sometimes seemed, I can assure you," I said. "The antics of a lunatic are a natural ruse."

We hailed a passing cab now, which reined up, Tubby cramming himself in through the door like a stoat into a hole. "Merton's Rarities," I said to the driver. "Hurry!" He hi-hoed at the horses and off they went, throwing us both sideways, Tubby pinning me heavily against the wall. "The point is," I said, "if Bill drew such a map, and it's come to light, then we've got to take up the scent, or we'll lose it again."

"The scent of *what*, Jack? *That's* the salient point, you see."

"A lost object. It was what you might call…a device," I told him.

"Ah! A *device*. Just so. For spinning straw into gold, perhaps?"

One didn't keep secrets from one's allies, especially from a man like Tubby Frobisher, who did as he would be done by, so to speak. "You recall the so-called Yorkshire Dales Meteor?" I asked.

"Plowed up a meadow owned by a country parson, didn't it? Burnt a hedgerow. There was some element of it that made it worth the attention of the press for a day or two. I seem to recall a ring of floating cattle roundabout a manure dump, although it might have been floating swine."

"It was the murder of Parson Grimstead that attracted the press. They were more or less indifferent to the flaming object—not a meteor, I can assure you. The Parson found a strange device, you see, in his cattle enclosure, and he hid it in his barn. He suspected, probably correctly, that it wasn't…of earthly origin."

Tubby gave me a look, but he knew enough about St. Ives's adventures over the years so that the look wasn't utterly dubious. "The Parson sent word to St. Ives," I said, "whom he had known man and boy, and St. Ives flogged up to Yorkshire to arrive the following morning, only to find the Parson dead on the ground inside the barn door. He was carrying a fowling piece, although he hadn't apparently meant to go hunting, at least not for birds. There was no sign of the device. A local farmer had seen a wagon coming out of the Parson's yew alley before dawn, driving away westward. It turned out that the device had been spirited away to the Carnforth Ironworks. According to a worker, a container of wood and iron had been built to house it, the interior of the container sealed with India rubber. As for the floating cattle, St. Ives found the report vitally interesting, but to my mind it simply encouraged the press to make light of a good man's murder."

"*Spirited away?*" Tubby said. "*Built to house it?* By whom?"

"You know by whom, or can guess."

"Ignacio *Narbondo?* What does he call himself now? Frosticos, isn't it?" He was silent for a moment. "We should have fed him to that herd of feral pigs when we had the chance. We'll add that oversight to our list of regrets."

Fleet Street was annoyingly crowded with evening strollers, and we crawled along now, the cabbie shouting imprecations, our pace quickening again as we rounded onto Upper Thames Street toward the Embankment. "The map, then?" Tubby asked. "You must have found this device and then—what?—lost it again?"

"Just so. What happened," I told him, "was that we three took the device out of the Ironworks under the cover of night, St. Ives, old Bill, and myself. We were waylaid near Silverdale at low tide, and Bill set out across the sands alone with the wagon despite St. Ives's reservations. He had the idea of fleeing into Cumbria, going to ground, and waiting for us to catch up. If the wagon became mired in the sands, he would draw a map of its exact location, although the odds of our recovering it were small. The virtue was that the device would be out of the hands of Frosticos, who would surely misuse it, whatever it was."

"It had a use, then?"

"Apparently, or so St. Ives suspected. The long and the short of it is that Bill disappeared. We fear that he went down into the sands somewhere in the vicinity of Humphrey Head. Did he draw his map? We didn't know. All these years we've assumed that the map, if there was one, sank along with the wagon and poor Bill."

"And so ends the tale," Tubby said. "Your device is lost, and two dead men to show for it."

"One last, salient bit. Merton, you see, frequents the Bay, where he has family, and years ago St. Ives asked him to be on the lookout for anything remotely relevant to the case. Lost things turn up, you see, sometimes, along the shore, sometimes in dredgers' nets. This is our first glimmer of hope."

"Well," Tubby said gloomily, "give me a kidney pie and a pint of plain over a glimmer of anything, especially if it's buried in quicksand." But Tubby was always a slave to his stomach, and there he was sitting beside me in the cab as we reined up in front of Merton's, game as ever.

Merton's Rarities, very near London Bridge, is part rare book shop, part curiosity shop, and a sort of museum of old maps and arcane paper goods, scientific debris, and collections of all sorts—insects, assembled skeletons, stuffed creatures from far and wide. Where Merton finds his wares I don't know, although he does a brisk trade with sailors returning from distant lands. In his youth he worked in the stockroom at the British Museum, where he established a number of exotic contacts.

The shop was well lit despite the hour. Tubby and I hesitated only a moment in the entryway, spotting St. Ives and Hasbro bent over the body of poor Merton, who lay sprawled on the floor like a dead man. Roundabout the front counter there were maps and papers and books strewn about, drawers emptied. Someone had torn the place up, and brazenly, too. Merton's forehead was bloody from a gash at the hairline, smeared by the now blood-stained sleeve of his lab coat. Hasbro was waving a vial of smelling salts beneath Merton's nose, but apparently to no consequence, as St. Ives attempted to staunch the flow of blood.

"Back room. Wary now," St. Ives told us without looking up, and Frobisher, no longer mindful of his kidney pie,
plucked a shillelagh out of a hollow elephant leg nearby.
He had the look of a man who was finally happy to do
some useful work. I took out a leaded cane and followed
him toward the rear of the shop, where we came to an
arched door, beyond which there was a vestibule opening
onto three large rooms: a book room, a storage room full
of wooden casks and crates, and a workshop. The book
room was apparently empty, although the storage room
afforded a dozen hiding places. "Come on out!" I shouted,
brandishing the cane at the shadow-filled room, but I was
met with silence.

Then Tubby called out, "He's bolted!" which didn't
altogether disappoint me. I found Tubby in the workshop, where a door stood open beyond a row of heavy
wooden benches littered with half assembled skeletons.
We looked out through the door, discovering a pleasant,
walled garden with a paved central square surrounded by
shrubbery. An iron, scrollwork table lay on the pavement,
its feet pushed into the shrubbery along the wall, which
the attacker had no doubt scaled, kicking the table backward when he boosted himself onto the copings.

We set the table up, which was very shaky, I might
add, with a treacherously loose leg, and while Tubby held
it steady, I climbed atop it and looked up and down the

empty by-street, which dead-ended some distance up against a shuttered building. It lead away downwards towards the river, winding around in the direction, roughly speaking, of Billingsgate Market.

"Gone," I said out loud. "No sight of him." And I was just leaning on Tubby's shoulder to climb back down when I saw a boy come out of an alley down across the way. He stood staring at me, as if trying to classify what species of creature I might turn out to be. To my utter surprise, he headed straight toward me, waving a hand in the air. —⌀

Chapter 2

What Happened
to the Map

"WHAT'S *THIS* NOW?" I said, and Tubby, still holding steady, said, "Enlighten me," with a good deal of irony, as if he was miffed that his only useful business was to anchor the table while I took in the view.

"Begging your pardon, sir," the boy said, breathing heavily. "There was a man came over this wall. I seen him."

"How long back?" I asked.

"Not ten minutes, sir. I followed him down toward the market, but lost sight of him. I thought at first he'd taken an oars downriver, but then I saw him duck into a gin shop, what they call the Goat and Cabbage."

"Send the boy around to the *front*," Frobisher said a little pettishly. "I'm not a damned *pi*laster."

"Right," I said, and was about to convey the suggestion when the lad took a mad run at the wall, sprang up, latched onto the copings, and heaved himself over, landing on his feet like a cat.

Tubby shouted and trod back in astonishment, letting go of the table, which toppled sideways, pitching me into the rock roses, thank heaven, and not onto the paving stones. It was the boy who helped me to my feet, dusting off my coat and asking was I injured, which I said I was not, although I gave Tubby a hard look for shirking his duty with the table. The boy might have been twelve or thirteen, and was in need of a haircut and a new pair of trousers a good three inches longer than the pair he wore.

"Finn Conrad, at your gentlemen's service," he said, holding out his hand, which I shook heartily enough. I immediately liked the look of the boy, who reminded me a little of myself at that age, but with considerably more gumption.

"Jack Owlesby," I told him. "And this is Mr. Frobisher. They called him Pilaster Frobisher out in India, where he spent a great deal of time in the sun. If you'd just lead the way inside, Mr. Frobisher."

"It's a pleasure to meet you, young comet," Tubby said to the boy, bowing in his portly way and shaking the offered hand before heading in through the open door "I'm speaking to an acrobat, I don't doubt?"

"Duffy's Circus, sir, born and bred. But I ran away two years back, after my old mother died, and I've been living hereabouts since, making my living in what way I can. Are these your whacking sticks?" he asked, gesturing, and we said that they were. He collected the leaded cane and shillelagh where they lay atop the workbench, surveyed the bones and skeletons as if they were pretty much what he expected to find under the circumstances, and went on into Merton's like an old hand.

Merton wasn't dead, thank God, but was sitting in a chair now, in that comfortable little browsing parlor he's got at the front of the shop. He held a glass of brandy and wore a bandage round his forehead. St. Ives and Hasbro sat opposite, and Tubby and I took the two remaining chairs. Through the window I could see London Bridge. Upriver lay the Pool, the masts of the shipping just visible, and faint on the air you could hear bells and whistles and other sorts of nautical noise. "I saw his face clearly," Merton was saying to St. Ives. "It was a broad face, nose like a fig and small eyes. Not a dwarf, mind you, but a small man. Apelike is the word for him. Quite horrible in appearance."

"In a brown coat," young Finn said, "begging your pardon, sir, and a watch cap. That's the very man I was telling these gentlemen about."

"What have we here?" St. Ives asked.

"Finn Conway, sir, at your service. I seen him come over the wall out back. 'What's this now?' I asked myself. Why would a man come over a wall when there's a door out front unless he's up to no good?"

"Quite right," Tubby said.

"He didn't see me," Finn said, "because I didn't want him to. He headed straightaway toward the river with me following after him, and went into a gin shop in what they call Peach Alley."

"The Goat and Cabbage," I said helpfully,

"That's the one. I took a look inside, nonchalant like, but I didn't see him. Maybe he's gone on through, I thought. There's a lot of what you might call *passages* down along there by the river. I waited for a bit, thinking he might come out from where he'd gone, but then a man came in and told me to clear out."

"Can you take us there in the morning?" St. Ives asked, and Finn said that he could, and then assured us that he could find very nearly anyplace a second time if he put his mind to it, just as easy as the first time. He had lived hereabouts long enough to know the riverside, he said, although he was presently without an address and was looking forward to summer and to less of this wind.

St. Ives asked him if he could find us a bite of supper, and sent him off with a handful of coins, considerably more money than was necessary, enough to tempt him if he were a rascally young hypocrite and not who he seemed to be, and in any event to get him out of the way while we reconnoitered.

"He'll be back right enough," Tubby said. "He's a game one. You should have seen him scale the garden wall, speaking of apes."

I could see that Merton was in a state, glancing fearfully about him as if at any moment his assailant might return to finish him off, but he calmed himself with an effort, and for the next quarter of an hour he laid out the facts as he knew them, and we pitched in with comments when we were able. Merton, it turns out, had been given the map by his uncle Fred, a sand pilot on Morecambe Bay who lives in the area of Grange-over-Sands. Fred takes excursions across the sands at low tide, Merton told us, out into the cockle beds off Poulton-le-Sands, or back and forth from Silverdale to Humphrey Head if the moon is right. Uncle Fred—a legend thereabouts—had been mired in quicksand, caught up by the incoming tide, run afoul of smugglers, and suffered all manner of perils and had lived to tell the tale. He wasn't one of the Queen's Guides, mind you, but that's what made him useful to certain people, especially that class of dredger who fished the quicksand by night.

Fred had found the map—it was as simple as that—near the top of the Bay. It was corked up in a bottle that had suffered some leakage. It looked curious to him, and he kept the map as a souvenir, putting it into a drawer and after a time forgetting about it. Then one day two weeks past he sorted out the drawer and found it again, and when Merton and he ran into each other at their Aunt Sue's house in Manchester, he gave it to Merton as a curiosity. Merton put it straight into the catalogue without a second thought, although he'd been cagey with the description, in case there was more to the business than met the eye. Then he sent up to Chingford-by-the-Tower to alert St. Ives.

"More *what* than met the eye?" Tubby asked, in his usual impatient way.

"The thing is," Merton said, "Uncle Fred talked the map around, you see, after he found it again in the drawer."

"Talked it around to *whom*?" asked St. Ives, looking at him narrowly.

"To the lads in a pub there in Poulton-le-Sands, over a pint, you know. Natural sort of thing, if you see what I mean, passing the time. Except there turned out to be two men sitting nearby, listening hard. One of them asked to see it, but Uncle Fred made up an excuse for not having it with him, although he did, right there in the pocket of his coat. He didn't like the look of either of them, and didn't know them, although he could describe them right enough. The one was a tall, scowly sort of fellow, swarthy, Fred told me. Unpleasant. A murderer's face, Fred called it. The other had dead white hair, and a face that looked as if it had been carved out of ice. There was something wrong with this second man that you couldn't quite name—Dr. Fell comes to mind. It was the tall man who did the talking."

St. Ives gave us a glance at this juncture. The detail of the white hair and the unnamable malevolence suggested that our man was indeed Ingacio Narbondo, now known as Dr. Frosticos, or sometimes Frost, St. Ives's longtime nemesis and the last man on earth I wanted anything to do with. He had gone out of our lives some time back— out of the world, I had hoped. His interest in the map would be as avid as that of St. Ives, although he would be considerably more ruthless in its pursuit.

"I take it that you saw these same men again?" Hasbro asked.

"Just the tall one," Merton said. "The first time was there in Manchester. Fred saw him on the street and pointed him out to me. He was loitering in a doorway and smoking a pipe. That could have been a coincidence, of course, or perhaps another tall man with similar features. We were on the other side of the street, you see, and it was evening. But then I saw him again, shortly after I was back in London, and no mistake this time. He followed me to the shop, and he wasn't clever at it either. Bold is the word for it."

"You're certain he followed you?" St. Ives asked.

"Yes," Merton said. "The second sighting there in Manchester might have been coincidence, but the third time always smells of a plot."

"And the white haired man?" I asked him.

"No. Only the tall one. The catalogue hadn't been distributed yet, but he asked straightaway to buy the map, said that he'd heard it had fallen into my hands. No pre-amble, no beating about the bush. 'I want the Morecambe Sands map,' he said."

"And you told him to bugger off," Tubby said.

"Not in so many words," Merton said, pouring him-self another glass of brandy. He swirled it in the light, looking shrewdly at us. "I played the fool, you see. Denied knowing anything about it. He accused me of lying, and I told him to get out. Then two days later there he was again, but with a copy of the new catalogue, Lord knows where he'd gotten his hands on it, which he laid on the counter along with the required sum, accurate to the penny. I told him I'd already sold it. He called me a liar, which of course was accurate, and walked out without being asked. I hoped that was the end of it."

"But he sent his simian cohort back in tonight and
bloody well took it," Tubby said.

"Ah! Ha ha! He *believes* he took it!" Merton said,
brightening up, but then shut his eyes and held his forehead with the pain of laughing, and it took him a moment
to get going again. St. Ives had a keen look on his face.

"Now, here's the long and the short of it," Merton
continued, looking around again, his voice dropping. He
tipped us a wink. "I *hoped* I'd seen the end of the gentleman, you see, and yet I'm a careful man. I set to work
and devised a false map on a piece of the same sort of
paper—but quite a different part of the Bay and with the
landmarks changed. Correct in all other ways. I doctored
the ink so that it ran, as if the paper had been soaked
in seawater, but not so much that the map couldn't be
made out. Then I colored it up with dyes made of algae
and tobacco and garden soil, and I slipped it into the box
under the counter, where I keep small money to make
change for the customers. Our man searched for it, as
you can see, throwing things around the floor. Then he
spotted the box, helped himself to the money, and found
the map. Of course I played my part. 'Take the money,' I
said to him, 'but for God's sake leave the other! It's of no
value to you.'" Merton sat back in his chair now, smiling
like a schoolboy, very satisfied with himself, but then his
face fell.

"His response was to hit me with a length of lead pipe. Quick as a snake. Perfectly unnecessary. I hadn't so much as twitched."

"The stinking pig," Tubby said, and of course we all voiced our agreement, but what I wanted to know was, what about the map, the real map? Merton had it safe as a baby, it turned out—rolled up, tied neatly with a bit of string, and thrust into the open mouth of a stuffed armadillo in the window. No thief, he informed us, would think to look for valuables inside an armadillo.

Merton leered at us for a moment, making us wait, and then said, "Fancy having a squint at it?" He was enjoying himself immensely now. He was resilient, I'll say that for him, but perhaps too enamored of his own cleverness, which the ancients warns us against. Still, he had done what he could to help St. Ives, and had nearly had his skull crushed into the bargain. He was a good man, and no doubt about it, and his ruse de la guerre seemed to have worked. He helped himself to a third glass of brandy, which he drank off with a sort of congratulatory relish before fetching the map out of the maw of the preposterous scaled creature nearby. He handed it to St. Ives, who slipped off the string and unrolled it delicately. After a moment he looked up at Hasbro and I and nodded. "It's as we thought," he said.

Just then the door swung open and Finn Conrad came in carrying meat pies and bottled ale, and, it turned out, most of St. Ives's money. St. Ives slipped the map into his coat while Finn set down his burden, handed back the bulk of the coins, and advised the Professor (begging his pardon for saying so) not to be quite so liberal with people he didn't know, not in London, leastways, although it mightn't be a problem in the smaller towns, where people were more honest, on the whole.

My appetite had fled when I saw Merton bleeding on the floor, but it returned now in spades, and that apparently went double for Tubby, who crushed half a pie into his mouth like an alligator eating a goat, and then settled back into his chair for some serious consumption, the rest of us not far behind him. Tomorrow morning, St. Ives told us, we would take a look into the Goat and Cabbage, if Finn would be so kind as to show us the way. Finn said that nothing would give him more pleasure, and then pointed out that someone should guard the shop tonight in Merton's absence, and much to Merton's credit he said that he would be quite happy if Finn would make up the settee in the workroom, and sleep with one eye open and one hand on the shillelagh in case the rogues returned.

"Out the back door and over the wall at the first sound of trouble, that's my advice," I told him, and Hasbro echoed the sentiment.

St. Ives was doubtful about leaving the boy alone in the shop at all, now that he knew something more of the men who possessed the false map.

"The stolen item," St. Ives said to Merton," "you say it's a...*satisfactory* specimen?"

"Oh, *much* better than satisfactory, I should say," Merton said, grinning. "*Considerably* better. Not that I claim to know anything about the art of...reproduction." He had been going to say "forgery," but there was no reason to utter the word with the lad standing by. *Reproduction* said rather too much, it seemed to me at the time. Certainly there was no profit, and perhaps some danger, in Finn's knowing things he didn't need to know. St. Ives, sensibly, brought the conversation to a close.

And so we locked young Finn safely into the shop and went out into the evening to see Merton home, where we delivered him safely to Mrs. Merton, he having fully recovered his spirits, and with an extra measure into the bargain. Mrs. Merton gasped to see the bloody bandage on her husband's head, but Merton was markedly indifferent to it. "Happy to be of service," he said to St. Ives, saluting. "I'll do my part!" We assured him that he already had and left him smiling gloriously on the doorstep.

In the morning Finn was already up and working when St. Ives, Hasbro, and I returned. Tubby had domestic duties and hadn't come along, which turned out to be to our advantage, given what happened later, although I'm getting ahead of myself. Finn had shelved the fallen books, made an orderly stack of the papers, swept the place out, and was soaking the blood out of Merton's lab coat, which, he said, wanted cold water and not hot so as not to "set the stain," which was something else he had learned during his years in the circus, where he had put in his time in the laundry. "All shipshape," he told us.

We breakfasted along Thames Street on kippers and eggs and beans, and then set out with Finn walking far on ahead, which was Hasbro's idea. No one would associate the boy with us, you see, when we were in the neighborhood of the Goat and Cabbage, and I was reminded once again that there might be some danger in our undertaking. To tell you the truth, it had begun to seem more like a holiday to me. —೧

Chapter 3

The Goat and Cabbage

L OWER THAMES STREET FROM the
Pool to the Tower is busy night and day, with
cargo coming off the ships and going onto them,
and shops open, and fishmongers hauling carts and
pushing hand barrows of whiting and oysters and plaice
and whelks toward Billingsgate Market, which smelled
of brine and seaweed and, of course, fish. All manner
of trade goods and all manner of people crept up and
down, jostling in and out of coffeehouses and shops,
intent on doing business or on getting in the way of
other people doing theirs. I was knocked sideways by a
grimacing man with an unlikely large and wet bag of
oysters over his shoulder, and knocked back again by
a donkey hauling a cart of herring barrels, but nobody

meant any harm and it struck me as rather agreeable than otherwise to be out and about on a busy spring morning, last night's blustery cold having given up and gone back to whence it came.

In all that seething crowd we lost sight of Finn, but then saw him again, lounging against a store front, eating something out of his hand, giving the last of it to a mongrel dog and setting out again without so much as a look in our direction, the dog at his heels. Half a block farther along, I smelled a waft of pipe tobacco, Sobranie again. The tobacco isn't all that rare, but it naturally put me in mind of the tall workman in Lambert Court last night. Then I thought of the small man who had been with him earlier in the evening, and then of Merton's description of his apelike assailant and of the tall man from the pub in Poulton-le-Sands, and suddenly, like a bonk on the conk, it didn't feel like a holiday any longer as the truth rushed in upon me. The two men in Lambert Court yesterday evening weren't the navvies they had appeared to be. One had evidently stayed behind to keep an eye on us, and the other had gone down to the embankment to beat poor Merton over the head with a pipe. Hasbro's untimely entrance must have complicated things for them, and yet they had managed to remain one step ahead of us.

Abruptly I wished I had taken along the leaded cane, and I looked around, trying to catch sight of the pipe smoker while I was revealing all this to St. Ives, who narrowed his eyes and nodded at me. But I saw no one who might be our man, or our men. Soon we drew abreast of a narrow alley that angled away toward the river. Finn was just then buying a bag of hot chestnuts from a man with a kettle on wheels, and he nodded discreetly up the alley, where there hung a weather-battered sign depicting the head of a goat wearing a cabbage leaf cap.

There was nothing for it but to push through the door into the fug of the gin shop, which was busy enough for that hour of the morning. A man was singing "Pretty Mary Tumblehome" in a voice like a broken cartwheel, and there was a good deal of low talk, which staggered just a little when walked in. It evened out again when we three trespassers had navigated the tavern and found calmer water in a corridor beyond.

There were a couple of straw pallets along the near wall of the first room off the corridor, and a chamber pot, and boxes of destitute old junk that you might see for sale in a two penny stall in Monmouth Street. Against the far wall stood a heavy oaken wardrobe with a broad, high door, considerably scarred and black with age—nothing that interested us in the least. We jibbed without a word, angling back out into the dark corridor, sailing past other dead-end rooms and none the wiser for any of it. Evidently we had come on a fool's errand.

"They'll no doubt find *us* soon enough," St. Ives said, shrugging, and he turned back down the corridor with us following, anxious to gain the street—or at least I was. But Hasbro stopped outside the room with the wooden wardrobe, cocking his head as if listening to something.

"Commodious wardrobe," he said in a low voice.

"Just so," St. Ives said. "Just so." He darted a glance up and down the corridor. "Jacky, watch the door," he whispered. "Give us a whistle if anyone appears."

But there was no need to whistle, because no one, apparently, was interested in us, a fact that had begun to seem peculiar to me. The entire mob had been aware of our entering the place. Someone, you'd suppose, would begin to wonder what we were about. I looked back to see Hasbro fiddling at the lock with a piece of wire and St. Ives endeavoring to see behind the wardrobe, which appeared to be pressed tightly against the wall, perhaps affixed to it. I wondered why the wardrobe would be locked at all, but just as the question came into my mind, the door swung open to reveal that it was utterly empty.

"Interior lock," Hasbro said, indicating an iron latch that was attached to the inside of the door, identical to and directly behind the outside latch. There was a key in it, which Hasbro removed and slipped into his pocket.

St. Ives reached in and pushed on the panel at the back of the wardrobe, fiddling with the mouldings, and very shortly the panel slid sideways to reveal a dark passageway beyond. Without an instant's hesitation St. Ives stepped through the door and ducked into the passage, waving at us to follow. I was quick enough to comply, half of my mind worrying that someone from the tavern would look in to see what we were up to, the other half worrying that they hadn't already done so.

I glimpsed a precipice ahead—stairs leading downward beyond a small landing, more or less in the direction of the river. St. Ives was already descending along a rusty iron railing. Hasbro followed behind me, swinging the wardrobe door closed, the passage instantly disappearing into utter darkness. I heard him step out onto the landing, and then the panel in the wall at his back slid into place with a clicking sound.

"Steady-on," St. Ives said from somewhere below.

There was a cool updraft, and a wet, musty smell that might have been the river itself. I heard what sounded like the roar and hiss of a boiler letting out steam. "Can you find your way, sir?" Hasbro whispered into my ear in a disembodied sort of voice.

I told him I could, and I stepped off, one foot in front of the other, gripping the railing with one hand and feeling my way along the wall like a blind man with the other, hoping that no rotten stair tread would catapult me into the abyss. Soon, however, I found that I could see tolerably well. There was light somewhere below, which brightened as we descended.

A vast room—more a cavern than a room—opened out, and we paused for a moment to take in the sight below us. The floor lay at a depth that must have been beneath or near the level of the river. On that floor lay two strange undersea craft set on stocks, one of them evidently half built. Roundabout them lay a litter of metal panels, casks of rivets, and heavy glass sheets in wooden racks. One of the ships was the length of a yacht, and might have been completely built for all I could see in that dim light, with a shape that reminded one of an oceangoing pre-historic monster—finny appendages and convex, eyelike portholes. The other vessel was smaller, just a shell, really, of a similar craft. Some distance away stood a third craft, exceedingly strange and unlikely, a sort of elongated orb standing on bent iron legs—apparently an underwater diving chamber. It had nothing of the diving bell about it, but was altogether more delicate, built of what appeared to be copper and glass, and probably capable of indepen-dent movement, if the jointed, stork-like legs and feet were any indication.

A few feet beyond that lay a broad pool of dark water, the lamplight glinting off little eddies and swirls on its

otherwise still surface, as if it were flowing eastward, perhaps a subterranean channel of the Thames, or a backwater of one of the underground rivers that transect the city—the Walbrook, perhaps, or a branch of the Fleet.

The ceiling soared away overhead, supported by arches of heavy, cut stone. There were gaslight lamps some distance up the walls, with iron ladders leading up past them to a web of narrow walkways. The walkways ran hither and yon far above our heads, linking platforms on which lay what appeared to be tools and crates, perhaps shipbuilding paraphernalia, too dim in the gaslight to make out clearly from where we stood near the base of the stairs. The platforms, evidently, could be raised and lowered: they dangled from heavy chains that angled away in a complicated, block and tackle system. The boiler and coal oven of an immense steam engine hissed and glowed beyond.

We were apparently alone in the room, and we descended the last few steps warily, the bottom stair-tread hanging a foot above the stone floor, held aloft by heavy chains suspended from above. The entire bottom flight shuddered with our movements like a ship in a cross sea. I was on the lookout for some sort of activity, and a little surprised (I speak for myself again) not to find any, especially with the boiler stoked and glowing. No one with legitimate business in this vast place would have any reason to hide. We were the intruders, after all, just as we had been intruders in the gin shop above.

St. Ives, however, didn't have the air of an intruder. He stepped down off the precarious stairway and walked eagerly to the half-built ship on the stocks. "A submarine vessel in the making!" he said, his mind instantly taken up with questions of science and engineering. He pointed at slabs of neatly stacked grey stone, weighted down by pigs of iron. The stone looked as if it had been cut out of blocks of sea foam. "Pumice," he said. "Do you see this, Hasbro? They've cut it into slices and encased it within the aluminium shell. Ingenious." He stood looking for a moment at a tub full of water nearby. Wires looped down into either end of the tub, dangling beneath floating rubber bladders with tubes running out of them. "They're producing hydrogen gas," he muttered, rubbing his chin. "I believe they're pumping it into the shell of the craft to further increase buoyancy. But what motive power? Electricity, surely, but what source...?" He went on this way, peering into recesses of the craft, talking mainly to himself, pointing out incomprehensible odds and ends, apparently having forgotten what we'd come for.

But what *had* we come for? If we were pursuing the simian man who had failed to steal Merton's map, we hadn't found any trace of him. Instead we had found a subterranean shipyard, very nice in its way, but another riddle, not a solution. I looked around warily, my mind far removed from questions of scientific arcana. I'll admit, craven as it sounds, that I was thinking of the potential for escape. Back up the stairs and into the Goat and Cabbage? The idea was almost welcome. At the down-river end of the cavern, I saw now, stood a pair of high doors, closing off an opening wide enough to cart in any sort of freight—the way in, no doubt. The wardrobe door was simply a bolt-hole.

And then something happened that was almost disorienting under the circumstances: I smelled pipe tobacco, faintly but distinctly. I looked around sharply, peering into the dim and distant recesses of the enormous room, but I saw nothing. My imagination? I heard a scraping noise from somewhere overhead, and I glanced up sharply at the walkways, where I glimpsed the small glowing circle of a lighted pipe. Someone leaned on a railing, looking down at us. He was tall man, I could see that much, and he was evidently in no hurry, but was considering us as if we were animals in a cage, which wasn't far wrong. The light was too dim for me to make out his features, but I knew well enough who he was. I saw a second man on one of the platforms now, also making no effort to hide.

"There they are!" I shouted, but my words were buried by the abrupt ratcheting, clattering sound of winches turning and of heavy chain hauled through iron rings and the whistle and gasp of steam. The entire system of chains and pulleys and winches seemed to be moving now, the cacophony erupting from far and near. The three of us turned as one back toward the stairs.

But the lower flight of steps was hovering some few feet above the floor, hauling slowly upward on its chains, already moving out of reach. We were trapped, just as I had feared. I realized with a cold start that my feet were wet. There was an inch of water on the floor now. Sluice gates—they had opened sluice gates. The dark river beyond the diving chamber had risen—was rising—and the truth, pardon me for saying it, flooded in upon me. We had been lured here, hoodwinked, the biter bit.

"The freight doors!" I shouted, probably worthlessly in that ongoing cacophony of noise, and I pointed wildly toward the distant doors and set out at a splashing run. Before I'd taken six strides, there was a hand on the back of my coat and I was stopped in my tracks, the water swirling around my ankles. I turned to see Hasbro gesturing in the direction of the diving chamber, which St. Ives was examining with a trained eye. *Of course*, I thought, wading after Hasbro, looking hastily into the maze of catwalks overhead, where the tall man still watched us. He was holding a rifle now, leaning casually against the railing as if he meant to shoot squirrels.

The ratcheting and banging ceased abruptly, throwing the room into an eerie silence but for the hissing of steam. There was a gurgling noise and a soft splashing of water as the tide rose abysmally fast—knee deep now, cold and dark as death. St. Ives had the hatch door open and was climbing in, one foot on the nearest outstretched, bent leg of the craft, his hand on an iron rung. He disappeared inside briefly, turned around, and looked out at us, leaning forward and waving me along, although I had no need of encouragement. I found the rungs easily enough, my hands made nimble by fear, to tell the truth. St. Ives ducked back into the chamber to allow me room to enter the surprisingly spacious compartment, where I slumped down on a padded bench and sagged with relief.

Hasbro's face loomed into view outside the hatch now, and I bent over to give him a hand in, hearing at that moment a small explosion—the crack of a rifle. Hasbro teetered backward off the rungs, holding on momentarily with one hand. I leaned out, grabbing for the lapel of his coat, but finding empty air, watching him tumble into the black water and disappear. St. Ives was so concentrated on the controls of the craft that he was oblivious, and I shouted incoherently at him, turning around and backing out into the open again, hunched up like a man trying to cram himself into a box, anticipating the bullet that would surely follow, and *did* follow. It glanced off the metal shell of the chamber near the side of my head, so close that I heard the ricochet along with the report of the rifle. ⁓

Chapter 4

The Bottom of the River

HASBRO LURCHED UP OUT of the flood, his hand gripping his upper arm, and I let loose of the rungs and splashed down alongside him, going under for one dark, cold, horrifying moment before getting my feet under me, river water streaming into my eyes, my clothes sodden. Hasbro waded forward, putting his hand on a rung and feeling blindly to get a purchase with his foot. He climbed heavily as I pushed from below, trying to keep at least partly protected by the curved wall of the diving chamber. St. Ives leaned out and hauled Hasbro in from above, and I scrambled up after him, finding myself inside for the second time, kneeling in a pool of water on the deck, gasping to catch my breath, and too stunned and flummoxed to know how cold I was.

The hatch was already slamming shut, but there was one last report from the rifle, only a dim crack, like two stones knocked together, and the sound of the bullet pinging off the interior walls of the chamber, four rapid, distinct *pings*, and then the flattened bullet dropping to the curved floor and sliding down into the shallow pool of water. I realized, as I plucked the spent bullet up from where it lay and put it into my pocket as a souvenir, that the chamber was illuminated now, a soft glow emanating from overhead lamps, and there was the sound of a beehive-like humming on the air.

St. Ives twisted closed the latch that secured and sealed the door from within, nodded his head with satisfaction, and said, "We're carrying dry cells! She's an independent traveler!" The statements meant nothing to me, but his apparent joy bucked me up just a little. He worked at the controls methodically, manipulating levers and wheels, cocking his head with concentration. I helped Hasbro off with his wet coat, the inside of which was a marvel of pockets. After he extracted a roll of bandage and a flask of the cask-strength malt whisky that he carried against emergencies of all sorts, he worked his shirt down over his arm, exposing the wound. The bullet had scored the flesh and then had gone on its way, thank God, although there was a prodigious quantity of blood, which we staunched with the steady pressure of a wet kerchief folded into a compress. Hasbro dribbled whisky over the wound and I tied it with the bandage, making a neat job of it. I was reminded of poor Merton, beaten bloody in his own shop. We were getting the bad end of things, and no doubt about it—apparently played for fools all along.

"Thank you, Jack," Hasbro said, offering me the flask. I raised it in a brief salute and took a swallow, nearly gasping at the strength of the whisky, and then gave the flask to St. Ives, who was smiling like a schoolboy. "Oxygenators," he said cryptically, nodding his head toward the controls. "Compressed air, so it's a limited supply, but it'll do if we look sharp. Jack, you'll be on call to let in fresh air when we need it—that lever on the port side, there. But be as stingy as a landlady with it." He turned the air lever downward, and there was a sort of metallic swishing sound, air through pipes, the exhaled air tasting cool and metallic.

St. Ives took a quick drink from the flask before handing it back to Hasbro and turning again to his work. Hasbro followed suit and then slipped the flask back into his coat. I won't say that we felt like new men after the whisky, but at least not so old fashioned as we had felt a few minutes earlier. There was a constant hum and mutter and whoosh now, the chamber having become a living creature. St. Ives turned to us and nodded, as if to say, "What about *that?*" and with Hasbro attended to and apparently well, there was nothing to be done but to let St. Ives go about his able business, and I for one was happy to let him do it.

I watched the water creep up the side of the heavy glass portholes, my mind beginning to turn, trying to come to grips with what this meant, this watery entrapment. We had neither food nor drink, aside from the flask. Perhaps, I thought, we could wait until the water reached its zenith and then open the hatch, flood the sphere, swim to the surface, and try to find our way up the stairs, which might be reachable in the high water. Or might not. And of course our friend with the rifle might simply be waiting for us, conspicuously closer now on his perch overhead, which would make matters difficult indeed.

My spirits declined even further when I suddenly recollected Finn Conrad emerging from across the way last night at the precise moment that I was surveying the street. I wondered, perhaps unkindly, whether the boy hadn't simply been waiting for us, whether he was an even better actor than he was an acrobat. It was he, I thought darkly, who had led us to the Goat and Cabbage, the Pied Piper turned on its head, and him cheerfully eating chestnuts outside on the street as we witlessly filed in through the door, avidly pursuing our doom....

The thing suddenly seemed to be a certainty, and that was a damned shame. I liked the boy, and I was shocked at the level of loathing I felt for scoundrels that would lure such a likely lad into a life of dishonor and falsehood. He had been monumentally helpful at Merton's, but now that seemed evidently suspicious. Of *course* he would have been helpful, if his goal had been to lure us into the gin shop, where we would almost certainly discover the secret door, one thing leading to another. He hadn't known about the map in the armadillo's mouth, I reminded myself with some small satisfaction: the vital secret was still safe. But then I recalled Merton uttering the word, "reproduction" in his enthusiasm last night, and my satisfaction fled.

I sat there with a heavy heart, with nothing to cheer me aside from the faded glow of the whisky, which had seemed sufficient only moments ago. But I sat so only briefly, because the water outside had risen beyond the tops of the ports and I found myself looking out into the inky black of subterranean water. Lamps came on outside the craft, illuminating things, and I saw fish—eels of some sort—darting away into the darkness. The chamber tilted abruptly, as if it wanted to float, and I shifted on the seat, trying to distribute the weight so that we didn't simply fall over like a dead thing.

"Hold on," St. Ives said, opening a valve and listening, his head bent and eyes narrowed. "I think I've…"

There was the sound of water rushing into what must have been ballast chambers, and we settled on the floor once again. St. Ives tentatively began to work the several levers that rose from the deck of the chamber, manipulating the thing's legs, the chamber rising and settling, pitching backward and forward in a way that was distinctly unsettling. I thought of an upended beetle, struggling to right itself, its myriad feet utterly useless to it, but I swept the thought away, aware that we were creeping along now with a slow, ungainly gait. "A drop of air, Jack," St. Ives said, and I dutifully let in a few seconds' worth.

"Where are we bound?" I managed to ask after I had done my duty. We could hardly climb the stairs, after all, and merely creeping about the floor of the shipyard would accomplish little.

"Out," St. Ives said. "We're bound for points east. It's my idea that we have no choice but to make away with this marvelous craft. We'll borrow it, I mean to say. If we could find the owner and ask permission, we'd do it, but under the circumstances it's quite impossible, ha ha. And of course we have immediate dire need of it, which justifies our actions somewhat." He furrowed his brow and shook his head, as if this were a thorny moral issue, but it was evident that he was elated, that he couldn't have asked for a more suitable answer to our dilemma.

The elation faded into puzzlement, however, for right then the water outside our craft was illuminated far more brightly, and a large, moving shadow hove slowly past. It was the submarine that had sat on the stocks, suddenly alive now, making its way out of the flooded cavern. We watched in mute astonishment as it passed slowly by, one of the lighted portholes revealing the frozen profile of Dr. Hilario Frosticos himself, clearly having been aboard all along, waiting in the darkness. He was sitting at a desk in a cabin full of books and nautical charts, looking down at some volume as if unaware of our existence. And in the moment before he and his submarine passed out of sight into the depths, he glanced sideways into a cheval glass that sat before him on the desktop, and I saw his abominable reflection staring back at me, his ice-white visage perfectly composed and disinterested.

The lighted portholes winked out one by one, as if he were passing beyond the wall of the cavern into a subterranean sea, and abruptly we toppled forward, off the edge of the shipyard floor, descending in a rush of bubbles, swept along in a current that bore us away eastward, as St. Ives had promised. The only illumination came from our own craft now, but I thanked God for it, underwater darkness filling me with a certain horror. More eels

undulated past the portholes, and a school of small, white
fish, and then a corpse floated past, bloated and pale, its
sightless, milky eyes staring in at us for a long moment
before it was swept away in a current. It was horrible, and
yet I scarcely remarked it, my mind still dwelling on the
submarine and the living, corpse-like man who navigated
it. Where had it gone, I wondered, and why had Frosticos
allowed us our freedom, if indeed he had?

The water slowly brightened roundabout us. St. Ives
switched off the lamps both inside and out, so as not to
waste power. If we were tethered to a ship, he pointed
out, then the ship's engines would generate abundant
electricity, but we depended upon the batteries—what
he had meant by *dry cells*—which were an unknown
quantity. We discovered ourselves to be in the depths
of the Thames itself, the water murky with silt and river
filth. How far we had come in the darkness we couldn't
say. Our rate of travel was mere speculation. It had no
doubt been equal to that of the river, but where in the
river were we?

It wouldn't do, St. Ives said, to surface in the Pool, or
in some other part of the river busy with shipping, and run
afoul of a ship's hawser, or come rushing up from below
to tear a hole in a ship's bottom. And of course as long
as we were afloat, we traveled at the whim of the current,
whereas we had some hope of controlling our movements

if we could find the bottom in still water. How to accomplish this feat—that was the thorny problem, although St. Ives had clearly taken it up as a challenge. We clanked into something unseen, spun slowly, and continued on our way. I let in another burst of air. Through the port I could see what must have been the remains of a wrecked coal barge slide past, and I realized that all manner of debris lay on the river bottom, most of it half buried in muck. It would have made fascinating viewing, no doubt, under different circumstances.

St. Ives allowed more water into the ballast tanks, and we sank again, settling momentarily, a cloud of mud rising around us and obscuring our sight. We found ourselves toppling forward as the river pushed against us, and it was only by flushing water out of the ballast tanks that we managed to right ourselves once more, bobbing along eastward again, careening this way and that way in a manner that was soon sickening, as if we were afloat in a laundry tub. I let in more of our precious air, which we seemed to be breathing up at a prodigious rate. Directly after that we were cast in shadow, a shadow that stayed with us for some time before passing on.

"A ship," St. Ives said, looking upward through a port. "Out of the Pool rather late." He took his chronometer from his pocket and peered at its face. "The tide is making, or nearly, if I'm not mistaken."

"Yes, sir," Hasbro put in. "Just past midday, given the moon's activities."

"Excellent," St. Ives said, winking at me.

I nodded my hearty assent, although truth to tell I know little about the tides. What I cared about at that moment was for the craft to cease its constant, rollicking, drunken behavior.

"We'll have a period of slack water soon," St. Ives told me by way of explanation. "Enough time, I very much hope, to find our way out of the river, ideally downstream some small distance, where we'll cause less of a sensation. Air, Jack."

"But when the tide turns," I said as I reached for the lever yet again, "won't that merely propel us back upriver?" I recalled the corpse that had visited us earlier. Quite likely it would continue to navigate the same shoreline, upriver and down, at the whim of the tides and with no end to its travels until it simply fell apart or was hauled in by a dredger's net.

"Absolutely," St. Ives said. "It won't matter to us, though. Don't give it a second thought."

"Ah?" I said, wondering at this. Certainly it *seemed* to matter.

"We'll be suffocated before the tide flows again," St. Ives assured me. "Almost without a doubt. There's no telling how much air we've been blessed with, but even if the tanks were full, with three of us breathing up the surplus we'll be dead as herring in a couple of hours. You can bank on it."

This silenced me, I can assure you, although St. Ives hadn't meant for it to. He was merely making a practical observation. For another half hour or more we floated and bumped and spun our way downriver, in and out of the shadows of moored or passing craft. I found that I had become unnaturally conscious of my breathing, and so I began breathing unnaturally, gasping now and then with no provocation, mimicking the wheezing of the air in the pipes. What had seemed a spacious chamber had shrunk to the size of a pickle barrel, and I fidgeted about, trying to occupy myself by peering out the ports, spotting no end of mired flotsam—a wagon wheel, a tailor's dummy, a chest half buried in silt and enticingly bound shut with heavy rope, probably containing gold coins and Java pearls the size of goose eggs, but already disappearing behind us.

"Air, Jack."

It seemed to me that the rush of air was labored now, as if the pressure were low. But I was distracted from that frightful thought when I became aware that we were slowing settling again to the bottom. River mud swirled up around us so that for a moment we could see nothing at all. St. Ives consulted a compass among a small array of instruments, and when the murk settled he pointed out a long, curved wooden beam, a ship's keel perhaps, lying half exposed on the river bottom. "That's our bearing," he said. "Along the edge of that beam. Due north."

He began to manipulate the motivating levers once again, carefully now, waiting for the muddy water to clear time and again to get a view of the sunken keel so that we could take another creeping step. We edged around impediments sideways, like a crab, and two or three times backed away from a cavernous sort of rocky pit. Twice we mired ourselves in weeds and had to tug ourselves free. The broken end of the keel was far out of sight behind us now, and St. Ives was navigating by compass alone, adjusting and readjusting our direction of travel, none of us speaking or moving more than was strictly necessary. How much time passed, I couldn't say, nor could any of us guess whether we were twenty feet from shore or sixty, whether we would creep out onto dry land, or bang up against the base of a cliff and find ourselves no nearer salvation than we ever were.

Again I opened the air valve, but the flow was feeble, a tired hiss, and the air in the chamber was distressingly thick. I tried to distract myself by watching our progress, but it was too frustratingly slow, and there was little of interest to be seen in the river, which was perpetually murky now in the slack water. Hasbro, who had either been asleep or in deep meditation, said, "I beg your pardon, sir?" and I had no idea what he meant until I heard the echo of my own voice in my ears, and I realized that I had been talking out loud, like a mad man, and with no idea what I had said.

"Nothing," I told him with the rictus of a smile. "Just musing."

"Best not to talk at all," St. Ives said.

I decided to try closing my eyes, but despite my best efforts, I couldn't rid my mind of the watery clanks and thumpings that accompanied our slow progress across the bottom of the Thames. Abruptly there came into my mind the morbid notion that I was nailed into a coffin and had been dumped into the sea, and that I was suffocating in the darkness. My eyes shot open and I sucked in a great gasping breath of air, but there was no nourishment in it, and I sat there goggling like a rock cod drawn out of deep water.

"Are you quite all right, sir?" Hasbro asked.

I nodded a feeble lie, but noticed through the port just then that bits and pieces of floating debris had apparently begun swirling past us from downriver, and that the clouds of silt were clearing much more quickly. I was filled with a sense of doom. We had missed our tide, it seemed to me, and I was persuaded that we should throw open the hatch and try our luck with the river, abandoning the loathsome chamber.... Hasbro, God bless him, handed me the whisky flask in that dark moment, and I took a grateful draft before handing it back to him.

Very shortly we began to make a certain haste over a flat and sandy bottom, and my spirits lifted. I was conscious of the water brightening around us, and up through the port I could see what looked like a silver rippling window, which must, I knew, be the surface of the river. Then the chamber was out into the atmosphere, the water level declining along the glass. We staggered ashore until we were waist deep and could go no farther. Gravity, St. Ives told us, had gotten the best of us as our buoyancy decreased, and we risked breaking our legs if we ventured onto dry land.

I swung out of the open hatch like a man plucked from the grave, and leapt down into the river as into a bath, inflating my lungs with air that was as sweet as spring water, splashing my way to shore like a frolic at Blackpool. Recalling that moment of freedom even now makes me wax metaphoric, although the memory fades quickly, and I'm reminded of how close I had come to shaming myself with my fears and my weaknesses. If I were a younger man today, with a more frail sensitivity, I might revise this account, and cast a more stoic light on myself, perhaps adding a small moment of personal glory. But be it only ink on paper, that would be to commit the same fearful folly again, and with a lie on top of it. Surely there's more virtue in the truth.

We had made our way, we soon discovered, to the lower edge of the Erith Marshes, almost to the bend above Long Reach. No one had seen us emerge—another bit of luck. Three hours later the diving chamber sat atop the bed of a wagon, affixed to a swivel crane and fenced in by empty crates to disguise its shape, all of it tied down securely and covered in canvas. We found ourselves on our way merrily enough, north to Harrogate now, where St. Ives told us we would replenish the compressed air at Pillsworth's Chemical Laboratories, and then on across the Dales and around the top of Morecambe Bay for a rendezvous with Merton's Uncle Fred at his cottage in Grange-over-Sands. We were in need of a sand pilot, you see, to go along with our map and our diving chamber. We had no time to waste if we wanted to catch the tide. —☙

Chapter 5

Hesitate and You're
a Drowned Man

W E HELD A SORT of council of war there in the wagon, mapping out our campaign so that we proceeded according to a stratagem rather than a whim. It seemed to us that the ruse with the map must have borne fruit. Surely there would have been some way for Frosticos to prevent our flight in the chamber if he suspected that we possessed the true map. He was sure of himself, apparently, and that was a solidly good thing. And yet if we were wrong in this notion, we dared not return to the Half Toad or to St. Ives Manor at Chingford-by-the-Tower, lest the Doctor's henchmen lurked about, on the lookout. We wanted simply to be quit of them, now that we had the means to make use of the map, and so we decided to make straightaway to Morecambe Bay in time to catch a particularly low tide. And yet we had some small matters of business in London, having to do with Tubby Frobisher, which I undertook to accomplish while St. Ives and Hasbro rattled away north with all possible speed.

It was an added bit of good fortune that Tubby could walk abroad without exciting the suspicions of our enemies, and could convey the tragic details of our untimely deaths to the newspapers, where he had a useful acquaintance who wrote for the *Times* and occasionally for the *Graphic*. It was reported that our diving chamber, with three suffocated bodies inside, had been washed up onto a rocky strand near Sheerness, where it was found by fishermen. The scientific community mourned: much lamented passing...eccentric genius...intrepid explorer, and so forth. St. Ives, vilified just months earlier over the incident of the burning squid, was lauded by paragons of science, and there was, Tubby informed us, talk of a bronze bust in a plaster niche at the Explorers Club.

It was all very gratifying, I can tell you. And of course before the news was revealed publicly, Tubby had looked in on Merton and then had scurried like Mercury himself down to Scarborough to alert Mrs. St. Ives and my own dear wife to the nature of the fraud. (Neither of them were quite as taken with our cleverness as they in all fairness should have been, we discovered later, especially when Tubby regaled them with his secondhand accounts of the flaming meteor over the Yorkshire Dales and the floating cattle and dead parson and other salient and half understood details.)

We knew little of this, of course, except that I had set Tubby into motion. It wasn't the first time, by the way, that St. Ives had been mourned, and I wondered whether it was a good enough ruse to further confound a man like Hilario Frosticos. But then perhaps he wouldn't need further confounding, since he already possessed what he understood to be Kraken's map. We would soon know, for better or ill.

———

St. Ives drove the wagon beneath a full moon, Hasbro and I sitting beside him, along a seldom-used dirt track that winds down from the forest below Lindale and carries on beyond Grange-over-Sands down to Humphrey Head, which was our true destination. We had ridden in secret along this same road a decade ago, engaged in a similar mission. That had turned out badly, as Tubby had pointed out, and taken all the way around we had fared scarcely better this time, at least so far, despite the success of our flight down the Thames and our subsequent hasty journey to the environs of Morecambe Bay.

The trees grew more stunted when we drew nearer the water, blown by sea winds as they were, and we found ourselves moving along at a slow pace, creaking over sea wrack and shingle covered with blown sand, the wind in our faces. The moon illuminated the road, thank God, or we might have met Kraken's fate, for there were innumerable creeks flowing out of Hampsfield Fell to the west, most of them half-hidden by dead leaves and low-growing water plants, and the place had a dangerously marshy quality to it that kept me on edge, ever on the lookout for bogs and sand pits. Several times we stopped to search out a crossing— ships timbers sunk into the mire—but midnight finally found us near the village of Grange-over-Sands.

The tide was turning by then, and we hadn't much time to lose, unless we wanted to wait another day for a second chance. But of course every hour that passed made it more likely that Frosticos would become aware of our little game with the forged map, if he weren't already aware of it. It was our great hope simply to avoid him, you see. Unlike Tubby Frobisher, we had no pressing desire to feed him to feral pigs or to anything else. We meant to keep him at a safe distance, smugly busy with his own fruitless search, never knowing that we were still pursuing the device in our own more useful way.

The moon was bright, and the broad expanses of infamous sand, cut by rivulets of seawater, appeared to be solid, with shadowy hillocks and runnels that hadn't been visible an hour ago when we had first come in sight of the Bay. It seemed quite reasonable that a person would venture out onto the sands for a jolly stroll, to pick cockles or to have a look at some piece of drowned wreckage that lay half buried off shore, only to have the place turn deadly on the instant, the tide sweeping in with the speed of a sprinting horse, or a patch of sand that had been solid yesterday, suddenly liquefied, without changing its demeanor a whit.

The opposite shore seemed uncannily near, although it must have been four miles away. We could see the scattered, late-night lights of Silverdale across what was now a diminishing stretch of moonlit water, and farther along the lights of Poulton-le-Sands and perhaps Heysham in the dim distance. There was considerable virtue in the clear, illuminated night, but an equal amount of danger, and so I was relieved when the track turned inward across a last stretch of salt marsh and away from the Bay, growing slightly more solid as the ground rose. We quickened our pace, climbing a small, steep rise, hidden by a sea wood now from the watching eyes of anyone out and about on the Bay.

Soon we rounded a curve in the track, and there in front of us stood Uncle Fred's cottage, which he called

Flotsam. It was very whimsical, built of a marvelous array of cast off materials that Fred had salvaged from the sands or had purchased from the seaside residents of that long reach of treacherous coastline that stretches from Morecambe Bay up to St. Bees, where many a ship beating up into the Irish Channel in a storm has found itself broken on a lee shore. Looking out over the Bay was a ship's quarter-gallery, with high windows allowing views both north and south. In the moonlight the gallery appeared to be perfectly enormous, a remnant of an old First Rate ship, perhaps, and it made the cottage look elegant despite the whole thing being cobbled together, just as its name implied. The cottage climbed the hill, so to speak, most of it built of heavy timbers and deck planks and with sections of masts and spars as corner posts and lintels. On the windward side it was shingled with a hodgepodge of sheet copper torn from ships' bottoms. It was a snug residence, with its copper-sheathed back turned toward the open ocean, and the sight was something more than attractive. There was a light burning beyond the gallery window, illuminating a long table already set for visitors. Someone, I could see, sat in a chair at the table—perhaps Uncle Fred, if he were a small man.

What amounted to something between a widow's walk and a crow's nest stood atop the uppermost room,

giving Fred a view of the sands from on high. I noticed
a movement there, someone waving in our direction and
then disappearing, and the door at the side of the gallery
was swinging open when we reined up in the yard. I was
fabulously hungry, and weary of the sea wind and anxious to get out of it, if only for a brief time. Uncle Fred
stepped out with what turned out to be a boy following
along behind him.

"The ubiquitous Finn Conrad," St. Ives said, laughing out loud to see him there. I wasn't quite so pleased,
although I kept silent. I hadn't revealed my suspicions
about the boy to St. Ives and Hasbro, because, to tell you
the truth, I felt a little small about doubting him. If he
was who he appeared to be, then I was a mean-spirited
scrub. If he was an agent of Frosticos, then I was a fool,
and perhaps a dead fool. But what on earth was he doing
in this out of the way corner of the Commonwealth? I'm
afraid I stood staring at him, dumfounded.

Finn nodded at us, touched his forehead in a sort of
salute, and said he hoped we were feeling fit. "I'll see to the
horses, sir," he said to St. Ives. "I rode bareback in Duffy's
Circus, before they sent me aloft. Three years as stable
boy." He took the reins and led the horses around out of
the wind, strapping on feedbags with an easy confidence.

It turned out that Finn had brought with him a
letter of introduction from Merton, in order to "set

things up," as Merton had apparently put it. Finn had traveled into Poulton-le-Sands by any number of conveyances, and then had come around over the bridge with a kindly farmer before making his way down the north side of the Bay on foot, having run most of the distance. He would have crossed the sands if the tide allowed, he said, in order to do his duty. St. Ives said that he very much believed it. I believed it, too, but his duty to whom?

Merton had been expansive in his letter, the incident at the shop seeming to be a rare piece of theatre now that he was removed from it. He laid out the details of the hiding of the map, the production of the forgery, and an account of St. Ives's eagerness to search for whatever it was that had gone down into the sands all that long time ago. There was a mention of the timely appearance of young Finn, whom he recommended without reservation. Even the armadillo made its appearance upon the stage. Uncle Fred, in other words, was *in the know*, as the Americans might say. Who else? I wondered darkly. But soon we found ourselves in the lamplit cottage looking at a joint of Smithfield ham, boiled eggs, brown bread, a pot of mustard, another of Stilton cheese, and a plate of radishes.

"You gentlemen have your way with that ham and cheese," Fred told us, rubbing his hands together as if he were even more pleased than we were, "and I'll fetch us something to wet our whistles."

"Amen," I said, my doubts abruptly veiled by the sight of the food, and it was fifteen minutes before we slowed down enough to say anything further, when Fred abruptly announced that it was time to go.

He looked remarkably like Merton, but not half so giddy. There was an edge of authority to him that made you think of a ship's captain—something that came from a lifetime of dangerous work in the open sea air, I suppose. Merton had revealed to us that his uncle had lost three people to the tide in the early days, and that he had lost his complacency at the same time, as he watched them being swept away into deep water, and he standing helplessly by. He wasn't a large man, but there was a keen, wind-sharpened look in his eye, and he was burnt brown by the sun. I found that I was heartened by his rough-and-ready presence. He listened as St. Ives told him what we meant to do, his eyes narrowing shrewdly. His nephew's letter hadn't mentioned the diving chamber, but had revealed only that we would want a pilot. It was the diving chamber that threw him.

"It's madness," he said. "You'll join the rest of them at the bottom of the sands."

"Almost without a doubt," St. Ives said, sitting back in his chair. "Clearly we need your help with this."

"You'll need help from a more powerful personage than Fred Merton," he said.

"Granted," St. Ives told him, "but Fred Merton is the one man on Earth that we *do* want. We'll trust to providence for the rest."

Fred sat silently, watching out the window, where the wind blew the sea oats and the moon shone low in the sky. "You mean to captain this vessel?" he asked St. Ives, who nodded his assent. "And you," he said to me, "you'll go along as crew?"

The question nearly confounded me. Fear, still dwelling in my mind from our previous jaunt in the chamber, showed me its ugly visage. Another moment of hesitation, and that visage would be my own. Finn was a youngster, of course, and St. Ives wouldn't consider his going along, not under these circumstances. Hasbro's arm was still tied up in a sling.... I nodded my assent as heartily as I could.

Fred stood up abruptly from the table, checked his pocket watch, and nodded toward the door. The rest of us followed him out into the wind, which was sharply cold after the comfort of the cottage. Finn brought the horses around, an enviably game look on his face, and he clambered up onto the seat, holding the reins. We cast off the tarpaulin and saw to it that all was shipshape with the chamber and crane and the crane's mechanical apparatus—a block and tackle rig running through a windlass mechanism with a heavy crank. It was double-rigged, and would allow for the separate lowering and raising of the diving chamber and a grappling hook. Our duty if we found the box was merely to grapple onto it securely, and then to stand aside and let the power of the windlass haul it out.

"Once we're out onto the sands," Fred said to us, "the full ebb will leave us high and dry. It'll be warm work then, because when the tide returns, it'll be with a vengeance. When I say we pack it in, that's just what we do, quick like. Hesitate, and you're a drowned man. Do you hear me, now?" He looked at each of us in turn, as if he wanted to see in our faces that we would obey the command. I answered, "aye!" and nodded my assent heavily, becoming a drowned man not being one of my aspirations.

We set out at once, Uncle Fred and Hasbro in a two-wheeled Indian buggy going on ahead, and the rest of us in the wagon, with Finn handling the reins. The track along the edge of the sands was solid enough out to Humphrey Head, which is a small, downward-bent finger of land smack in the center of the top of the Bay, covered with grasses and with stunted trees growing on its rocky, upper reaches. It afforded us no shelter at the edge of the sands, either from the wind or from the view of others out and about on the Bay, and of course there was no time to concern ourselves with these "others," in any event.

The tide was still declining, and as it withdrew it revealed surprisingly deep and narrow valleys as well as broad sand flats, the water vanishing at a prodigious rate. Entire shallow lakes and rivers, shimmering in the moonlight, appeared simply to be evaporating on the night air. It was the sand flats that were worrisome, because they might be solid or they might be quick, the difference discernible only to the practiced eye of a sand pilot.

We left the buggy tethered to a heap of driftwood that stood well above the tide line, and straightaway ventured out with the wagon, Finn still driving, Hasbro up beside him, and Uncle Fred walking on ahead, prodding the sand with a pole to be doubly sure, Kraken's map in his hand. Where was I, you ask? I was already ensconced in the diving chamber along with St. Ives. As you might have discerned, I had no desire to be there, and even less now that I was within that confined space, but either my natural timidity or what passed for courage still prevented my saying so. The hatch stood open to the night air, for which I was grateful. ⁐

Chapter 6

The Undersea Graveyard

W E HAD WANDERED A quarter mile or so out onto the sands when Fred once again stopped to study the map. Kraken had fixed the location of the sunken device by lining up a blasted tree above Silverdale with a chimney pipe atop a manor house beyond it and away to the northeast. Fred walked along a line defined by the tree and the chimney pipe until he was very near dead center on yet another pair of conspicuous points, the spire-like pinnacle of a high rock atop Humphrey Head, and a stone tower on a hill off in the distance toward Flookburgh. He gestured the wagon forward, stopping it a few short feet from the edge of what turned out to be a broad pool of quicksand.

"This is what we call 'Placer's Pool,' hereabouts," Fred told us. "It's always quick, never solid. A man named Placer and his bride went down into it in a coach and four, with their worldly goods, because they were in a flaming hurry and didn't bother to hire a pilot, but left it up to the driver to find a way. The fool found it right enough, but it wasn't the way they had in mind. If your man was bound from the shore opposite to Humphrey head, then..." He shook his head darkly. "The good Lord alone knows what you'll find down there, because no one else has stepped into Placer's Pool and come back out again."

It was then that I began to grasp the obvious truth, although of course it should have been plain to me all along: we weren't plunging into a pool of water this time, but into a pot of cold porridge, so to speak. It came into my mind simply to admit to St. Ives that I'd rather be pursued by axe wielding savages than to drop blind into a pool of quicksand, but I sat there mute, trying to distract myself with the goings-on outside, looking at the grappling hook where it dangled in the grip of one of the craft's pitiful claws. My mind argued senselessly with itself—whether it would be courageous to admit my cowardice and stay topside, or cowardly to *fear* admitting it, descend into the murk, and risk going insane. There would be no opening the hatch in these waters,

I told myself insidiously. I pictured Bill Kraken, hurriedly sketching his map in the moonlight, corking it up in a bottle, and heaving it end over end toward solid ground, and I very much hoped that there had been something in the bottle to drink before it became a mere glass mailbag.

But of course there wasn't a moment to lose. Fred looked at a pocket watch, shouted, "Thirty minutes by the clock!" and St. Ives shut us in tight. We were lifted bodily by the crane, Hasbro turning away with one arm on the windlass crank as if letting down an anchor while Fred held the horses steady. The sound of their voices and labor seemed to come from some great distance as we swung out over the pool of quicksand, me gripping the metal edge of the circular bench as if it were the edge of a precipice.

"Surely the tide won't return in a mere thirty minutes," I said to St. Ives.

"No, sir," St. Ives said. "But we must agree upon an absolute limit, you see. In thirty minutes we'll either have failed or succeeded. If we succeed, they'll drag the box out bodily with the crane. If we fail, they'll drag us out."

"Good," I said. "Good." In fact I liked this very much. *Thirty minutes*, I told myself. Almost no time at all…

The myriad sounds of the living chamber rose around us, and we began to descend, St. Ives sitting there mute, attentive to his business, not a furrow of concern on his brow. I was already in a cold sweat, trying to manage my breathing, sending my mind off to more pleasant, imaginary, places, only to have it return ungratefully an instant later, not taken in by the ruse.

Now there was nothing outside the ports but brown, mealy darkness, the wall of congealed sands illuminated by the interior lamps. Our tanks were full of ballast to hurry our descent, but even so we drifted downward very slowly, the sand shifting around us, gently disturbed by our passing, with suddenly clear windows of trapped water that closed again at once.

"Two fathoms," St. Ives said. And then after a time, "Three."

"What lies beneath us?" I asked, suddenly curious. I hadn't given any thought to our destination.

"Ah!" St. Ives replied, glancing at me. "That's an excellent question, Jack. What indeed? More of this quicksand, lying on a solid bottom, perhaps, in which case we've almost certainly failed unless we land square on the wagon, because our movements through this sand would be both sightless and slow." He shook his head. "Or it might be that…" He paused now, staring hard through the port, where there had floated into view the face of a wide-eyed sheep, looking in on us with a certain sad curiosity. Most of it was invisible in the heavy sand, and we could make out only its ghostly visage. It appeared to be perfectly preserved in this dense atmosphere, or more likely only recently drowned. We seemed to draw it along downward for a moment, as if it heeded our departure, but then, like an image in a dream, it faded into the silent darkness overhead.

"Six fathoms," St. Ives said. "I believe we're descending more rapidly."

"The water seems to be clearing," I pointed out hopefully. "Do you see that broken oar?" It floated some distance away, a piece of an oar weighted down by an iron oarlock. At the depth of the sheep just minutes ago it would have been hidden from us. The sand swirled in an upward flowing current now, as if clear water were rising from beneath us. Then abruptly there was a clattering noise, something hitting the underside of our craft, and we emerged into water that was pellucid as a pail full of rain, and a sight that was utterly uncanny.

A small, upright wooden chair that our craft had apparently driven downward, now bumped and floated its way upward past the ports, and I peered out to watch its ascent. The sand layer hung overhead like a layer of thick clouds, and floating beneath it was a scattering of wooden objects, topsy-turvy chairs and tables from someone's drawing room, lost to the sands and now forever trapped beneath the heavy ceiling.

"We've come through the false bottom," St. Ives said, "at just over ten fathoms."

"The false bottom of what?" I asked, letting in a whoosh of air in through the pipes.

"The bottom of the *Bay*, Jacky. Into subterranean water. I've long suspected that there was communication between Morecambe Bay and some of the inland lakes—Windermere and Conniston Water, and perhaps north into the great lochs. There! Do you see?"

And indeed I did. An illuminated area of the actual seabed was clearly visible below us now, alive with great, feathered worms reaching out of holes in the sand, and colorful anemones the size of giant dahlias. A pale halibut, large as a barn door, arose from the bottom and winged its way into the darkness as if we had awakened it, and then a school of enormous squid slipped past, watching us with large eyes that reminded me of the face of the suspended sheep.

With a soft bump we settled into the sand, St. Ives attending to his levers, and almost immediately we were off, striding along on our crooked legs. St. Ives was surer of himself now, having honed his skills on the bottom of the Thames. "We've got about two hundred feet of line," he told me, "and so we're on a short tether. Some day we'll come back prepared to do a proper investigation… There's something!"

There was indeed something—what appeared to be a stagecoach of the sort you might have seen on the Great North Road a century past, when coaches were more elegant than they are today. It stood upright on the sands as if it were a museum tableau—a very dusty museum. The wheels were buried to the axles, the exterior covered with undersea growths—barnacles and opalescent incrustations, decorated by Davy Jones. The skeletons of four horses were tethered to it, and there were human skeletons inside, still traveling hopefully. Household objects littered the sea floor: pieces of luggage, crockery jars, broken crates spilling out bric-a-brac, porcelain vases, an iron teapot, a fireplace screen, bottles, a heavy crystal goblet half full of sand. A small bookcase miraculously stood upright, its glass doors unbroken, the books still standing on the shelves, held in place only by the rigid leather covers, the contents no doubt having melted into mere pulp like a lesson in humility. Fishes swam around and between the lumber of objects, enjoying their inheritance.

As the chamber strode shakily through this undersea museum it was easy for me too imagine what had transpired: the passengers, no doubt the Placer family, crossing the sands in order to avoid the extra few hours of travel around the top of the Bay. The weather had been fine, the sands apparently dry and solid. But then suddenly not

so solid—the wheels abruptly mired, the horses stumbling forward, sinking to their withers, thrashing to get out, but simply propelling themselves deeper into the mire, the passengers and the driver pitching the cargo overboard—anything to lighten the load, but all efforts utterly useless except to assure the victims that their worldly goods would be waiting for their arrival at the bottom of the sea.

It was St. Ives's notion that we were within a vast oceanic cave with a perforated roof, if you will, the quicksand pits created by upwelling currents, which accounted for the suspension of the sand particles and for the firm sand flats and cockle beds in the Bay above, which lay on solid tracts of seabed. There was something immense about the darkness that surrounded us, and it seemed quite possible that this hidden, underwater world, an ocean beneath the ocean, might pass well beyond the shoreline of Morecambe Bay.

And then we saw it: Kraken's wagon, gradually appearing within our halo of light. I had almost forgotten about it, so caught up was I with the strange nature of the dead place where we had found ourselves. The wagon was settled on a solid bit of sea floor, washed by currents. There was no skeleton, thank God, but that meant only that poor Bill's bones numbered among the billions scattered across the vast cemetery that is the World Ocean.

In the bed of the wagon, beneath a shroud of silt, lay the wood and iron strongbox that contained the device, whatever it was—something worth the death and injury it had engendered, I hoped.

St. Ives looked at his chronometer, and then immediately set to work with the levers that manipulated the grappling hook. On either side of the crate there were what appeared to be leather-covered chains that functioned as handles, and I watched as our mechanical arm extended, its claw reaching out with the hook.... Too far away. We crept closer, bumping up against the side of the wagon with a muted thud. Again the arm reached out.

I became aware of something then: a light in the distance, a bright, moving lamp. It looked almost cheerful in all that darkness, like the moon rising on a dark night, and it took my mind a moment to grasp the fact that it oughtn't to be there.

"The submarine!" I said, for what else could it be? No sooner had I uttered the words, than the craft turned, displaying its row of illuminated ports. I could make out the dark shadow of its finny shape. St. Ives had been correct. We were in a navigable, subterranean sea, apparently open to the pools or rivers we had encountered in the underground boatyard. Dr. Frosticos had found us.

"Can you discern what he means to do?" St. Ives asked, concentrating on his task.

"No. It's difficult to tell how far off.... Wait, I believe he's coming directly toward us now, moving slowly. Perhaps he's just seen us."

"We've got it!" St. Ives said, glancing through the port at the approaching submarine. He gave the grapple a small tug to assure that it was secure, and then tugged in earnest, and we teetered forward for one breathtaking, eye-shutting moment before we settled back onto our pins. The box slid neatly off the bed of the wagon in a silty cloud and settled on the sea floor, dozens of feather worms snatching themselves into their holes. St. Ives released the grapple, retracted the mechanical arm firmly against the hull of our craft, and began to propel the chamber a few paces off. "We'll leave the rest up to our friends topside," he said with satisfaction.

"Gladly," I said, glancing out through the port at the submarine, suspended there at a distance of perhaps 50 yards, although it was difficult to tell in the darkness. Frosticos seemed to be doing us the favor of casting a helpful light on our work.

"Keep an eye on that box, Jack," St. Ives said, looking steadily at his chronometer. "We should see Merton's hand at play right about...now." All was still for a moment, and then the box gave a jerk and began hopping and scooting along the floor of the sea, sand and sea bottom debris rising in a cloud. St. Ives nodded agreeably at me, and I couldn't help but smile back at him, our notable success having swept the fears out of my mind like yesterday's cobweb. All this time, of course, I had been doing my duty with the oxygen lever, and I noted cheerily that the air still whooshed briskly through the pipes. Suffocation, then, was still some distance off. We began our creeping, homeward progress, our real work finished. We simply had to wait our turn to be reeled in. St. Ives meant to be as directly under the crane as ever we could be, so that our ascent was unimpeded by anything but a floating chair or two.

I waved victoriously at the submarine, imagining happily that the good doctor's head was set to explode from frustration. The craft had by then begun to move away, and was circling around as if turning tail for Carnforth in defeat. "He's showing us his back, the dog," I said to St. Ives. "Slinking away." But the submarine continued to turn in a close circle, not slinking away at all, and soon the light was aimed dead at us, its watery glow obscuring the shadow of the ship behind it. Abruptly it launched itself forward, flying at us in an increasing rush. —☙

Chapter 7

The Turning of the Tide

I GASPED OUT A warning to St. Ives, who shouted, "Hold on!" at that same moment. He was bent over the controls, high-stepping our awkward craft across the sea floor now, attempting to maneuver us out of the way of the approaching submarine, which veered to remain on course. I held on with an iron grip, watching our doom hurtle toward us. The submarine easily compensated for our creaking, evasive ploys, and within moments we were blinded by the intensity of its light, and we both threw ourselves to the deck, hands over our heads, as if we could somehow protect ourselves.

The chamber toppled backward, and we were thrown together in a heap. I banged my elbow into something hard, but scarcely felt it, fully expecting the rush of cold water, the desperate, futile flight through the hatch. But there was no rush of water, and I had no sensation of our craft having been struck by anything. The light from the submarine was gone. The submarine had passed over us, and we found ourselves dragged along backward at what seemed to be a prodigious rate. It was our friends above, hauling us out bodily. We were "packing it in" as Fred had put it, right on time, and there was no dignity involved in the packing. I gripped the stanchions that supported the circular seat, and looked up through the port at the dark ceiling of our grotto, and once again I saw the flotsam held in stasis against the sands.

Then the blinding light again, and the submarine swept past, inches overhead, its dark shape passing like a great whale, and I thanked my stars that we were tipped flat, for the submarine evidently didn't dare to swim any closer to the sea floor. But my musings were shattered by a heavy jolt, and now out of the port I saw that we had bulled our way straight into the coach and four. A rain of human bones tumbled out through the window. Our retracted arm hooked into the bottom of a horse's skull, which sailed along with us like a misplaced figurehead before another jolt knocked it free. Then suddenly we were ascending smoothly, and we hauled ourselves gratefully onto the seats again, taking stock of bruises and abrasions.

We passed through the stasis layer into the murk of
the sands, St. Ives letting out ballast to aid our ascent,
and I reminded myself not to be quite so prematurely
satisfied in the future, gloating over a victory before the
enemy had left the field. Now we were clear, though.
He could hardly follow us into the pool of quicksand.
"Nothing broken?" I asked St. Ives.

"My chronometer, I'm afraid." He held up the shattered timepiece. "I'd rather break an arm, or very nearly.
But not a bad bill to pay, all in all."

We continued to ascend in silence for another minute
or two, but then abruptly stopped.

"Perhaps a fouled line," St. Ives said. "They'll be at it
again directly."

But the minutes passed, and still we sat there, my
mind turning in the silence. It came to me that I should
make a clean breast of my long-held suspicions while
I had a quiet moment. "I'm a little worried about an
element of this entire business," I said.

"Out with it, then."

"We've had some good luck," I told him. "And it seems
we've been clever. But consider this: what if Frosticos
knew what we were about, and I mean from the beginning. That business at Merton's—knocking poor Merton
on the head like that—what if it was meant to move us
to action? For my money Frosticos wasn't foxed by the

false map for more than a moment. He *knew* we had the original, and he intended for us to lead him to the box. He provided us the means by lending us this diving chamber. We were at the mercy of the tides once we arrived here at the Bay, and it was no great feat for him to lurk about the subterranean reaches watching for us when the time was right. Then he played a helpful light on our endeavors until we had succeeded, at which point he tried to murder us in cold blood, having done with us."

St. Ives sat thinking, but there was only one element of the theory that required any thinking. He reached up and gave us another gasp of air. "You say he wasn't foxed by the map," he said carefully. "You're suggesting…"

"I don't mean to *suggest* anything," I said, looking out into the by now thick sands, "only that we might have been played like fiddles."

"I sense that you don't want to cast any blame on Finn Conrad, but he might easily be the necessary link in the chain? His appearance outside Merton's was certainly convenient."

"It was," I said, "although it's as easily coincidental. Perhaps Merton's forgery was simply no good, and Frosticos saw through it."

"You've seen his handiwork," St. Ives said.

"Yes, but suppose Frosticos had come here straight-away by some subterranean route and had already found the map useless before our arrival, thereby suspecting it to be a forgery and lying in wait for us. When he saw us in our lighted chamber meddling on the sea floor..." I shrugged and gave us more air.

"But we've got to consider that Finn was our means of finding the boatyard and discovering this chamber. We were forced to flee in it in order to avoid drowning or being shot by men who seemed to have known we would come along when we did."

"One other thing," I said. "You were careful to slip the true map into your coat pocket, but Merton wasn't half so careful, especially with his insanely detailed letter, which he placed directly into Finn's hands before sending him post haste to the Bay."

"I find the idea distressing," St. Ives said wearily. "I don't say that I find it unlikely, just distressing."

"I've been distressed by it for the past days," I told him, "and I should have spoken up earlier. But I like the boy, and I don't want to malign him, especially when there's the chance that he's innocent. Perhaps we're as shrewd as we think ourselves to be, but it looks very much as if Frosticos has been leading us along like blind men." I watched the unchanging view through the port, worried that they were taking an infernally long time, and slightly unhappy with myself for having laid out my suspicions about Finn Conrad like a trial lawyer while insisting that I didn't want to malign him.

"For the moment," St. Ives said, "let's remember that all their machinations have been in vain. We'll keep a weather eye on Finn, just for safety's sake, but we'll not condemn him until we're certain."

"Good enough," I said, and abruptly we began to rise again, jerky and quick, and within moments we burst out into the dawn twilight, dripping watery sand, having been reeled in ignominiously, but alive. I saw straight off, however, that something was amiss.

The wagon was tilted disastrously, headfirst into the sand. Fred had untied the team, their forelegs covered with ooze, and was leading them away. Finn stood by him, but I saw that Hasbro lay over the back of one of the horses, unconscious or dead. Fred glanced back at us with concern evident on his face, and when St. Ives opened the hatch Fred shouted, "Remain *very* still, lads. Your friend's been shot. He'll live to tell the tale. There's nothing for you to do for him." He pointed up the bay before turning away.

We looked in that direction discerned movement atop a high dune not too far off the shore. It was impossible to say who it was for certain, but we had no doubt that it was our tall friend who had peppered away at us in the boatyard.

Then we saw that we hadn't, in fact, been drawn clear of the sands at all, but our legs and underbelly were still submerged. The wagon itself was half sunk, too, and Fred had evidently unhitched the team in order to save them from being drawn down with the wagon. The box was grappled to its line, and it seemed likely that the combined weight of the box and the diving chamber and we two human beings had been enough to haul the wagon down into the mire.

"One at a time, now," Fred shouted in a voice meant for the deck of a ship. "Out the door and across the wagon, lads. It's the only way. And be quick about it! Don't stand arguing." He set out toward shore.

"Out you go, Jack," St. Ives said, putting his hand on my elbow.

I shook it off. "You first. Think of Eddie and Cleo," I said to him. "And take the box with you or this is all for nothing. I'll follow."

Of course he started to protest, but I cut him off sharp.

"It's no good," I told him. "My mind's made up. So it's either out the door or shut the hatch."

Fred shouted something more from afar, shouted as if he meant it, and St. Ives shook his head darkly and swung carefully out of the hatch, reaching for the line along the side of the crane, stepping across to get a foot on the bed of the wagon. At once there was more shouting from without, and then the unmistakable sound of a rifle shot. I was thinking quite clearly and reasonably and was filled with a certain calm, and doubly determined to wait until St. Ives was clear of the wagon and the box with him.

He had his shoulder under it now, lifting it upward to take the weight off the grapple. When it was free, he carried it heavily to the rear of the wagon and set it down in order to drop to the ground. Beyond, nearly halfway to Humphrey Head now, the others swarmed along, Fred leading the horses with one hand, the other holding onto Finn's arm. I saw the boy look back at us, and Fred letting go of him for a moment to gesture for us to hurry. And in that moment Finn bolted, back across the sands toward us. Fred slapped the horses and sent them careening forward, carrying Hasbro toward high ground, and he turned and ran back after the boy. There was another rifle shot, and I saw Fred drop to the ground, but then he was up again and running.

I saw something else, too: far in the distance, out toward the broad ocean, the tide was returning. It appeared as a wall of roiling whitewater, lit by the rising sun. How high and how distant I couldn't make out, but it was moving toward us like galloping doom.

St. Ives saw it, too. He left the box on the bed of the wagon and ran toward Finn. What the boy thought he could accomplish returning to the wagon I can't say. The only answer was that he was coming to our aid at the peril of his own life, and I was filled with happiness and shame both. Even so, he had chosen the worst moment for his heroics.

I leaned out of the hatch in a fair hurry now and clutched wildly at the crane arm, managing to grab the grappling hook, looking back to see St. Ives stopping Finn in his tracks, urging him back toward shore. Holding onto the grapple, I stepped out across the three empty feet to the tilted bed of the wagon, and suddenly I was falling, the line reeling out of the unsecured windlass. I clutched at the air futilely with my free hand, landing on the sands without a shudder, plunging in knee deep. I could hear Fred shouting, and St. Ives shouting, and out of the corner of my eye I saw Finn catapult past St. Ives and run out across the sands. Fred grabbed St. Ives by the coat now and dragged him back bodily, and St. Ives had no choice but to follow. Together they fled toward shore, not knowing that I was mired and supposing that I would gather Finn up and follow.

I heard the ratchet sound of the windlass crank, and the rope, which was coiled atop the sand like a floating snake, began to retract. I held onto the grapple with both hands, otherwise keeping very still, and after a moment the line went taut, and I began to rise from the sands with the heavy sound of sucking and of gasping as my boots pulled free. I let go with one hand and reached for the side of the wagon, getting a good grip on it, kicking myself up onto the seat and clambering to the bed, where I stumbled to my knees, breathing heavily, half with fear and half with exertion. Finn had jumped down now, and was waving me on and pointing toward the tide, frighteningly close, moving in a long even mass of dark green and white.

Spurred by this sight, I leapt down, heeding Finn's admonition to run, but when I glanced again at the tide I saw that I could not. The quarter mile to shore was simply too far. Fred and St. Ives would be hard pressed to save themselves. To the north, the hillock of sand from which the doctor's henchmen had been shooting was empty. They'd seen the advancing sea and gone away like sensible men.

"To the wagon!" I said to Finn, and the two of us climbed back up onto the bed, which was canted steeply downward, its stern to the tide. Finn's face wore an avid sort of lunatic joy, as if this were an adventure rather than a death sentence. My own thoughts were equally lunatic— that the wagon might save us, and that I might save the abandoned device, which had taken a disastrous toll over the years. I was damned if we'd lose it now. I shouted at Finn to lash himself to the mast of the crane with the line from the grappling hook, and I picked up the box and staggered to the front of the wagon, where the diving chamber hung with its hatch open. I spun half around with the effort of throwing the box, nearly pitching off into the sands again, but I was dead on. It crashed through the open hatch, the ocean-corrupted case knocking itself to flinders, the device sliding beneath the seat.

When I turned around the Bay behind us was a shimmering, rapidly expanding sea, its leading edge billowing and surging forward at a height I wouldn't have thought possible, and I could do no more than throw myself down on the bed of the wagon and latch onto the crane mast like a limpet before the tide was upon us. The waters slammed into the wagon, throwing a wave of cold ocean across our backs at the same moment that it pitched the rear of the wagon upward and forward, so that it bucked like a spooked horse. I was flung into the air, but I hung on tenaciously, hearing the splintering of wood as the wheels and axle and tongue of the wagon were torn from the bed like rotten sticks. We spun around crazily, abruptly free of the quicksand, and I slammed down sideways to the deck again, aware that we were flying forward on the crest of the tide at a prodigious speed.

After a few moments, I realized that doom hadn't overtaken us after all, at least not yet, and I ventured a look around to see how things stood. What I saw was the oddest thing: ahead of us lay dry sand flats and dunes, cockle beds and half-buried debris, but beneath us the roiling tide was tossing and tearing along, now surging ahead as if to outrun us, now abating so that we moved ahead, careening along at the very forward edge of the rushing sea in a death-or-glory flight.

I heard Finn shout out loud, not a warning or a shout of fear, but one of primal joy as we sailed like maniacs up the Bay, bouncing and scudding on the current. I clung stubbornly to the crane mast, but Finn stood up and let go with one hand, holding on with the crook of his elbow, dipping and bobbing, loose-kneed and as sure of himself as if he stood bareback atop a horse, reeling around the center ring of Duffy's circus.

We were quartering across the Bay now, swept west as well as north, so that we would make a landfall somewhere above Grange-over-Sands. I espied the crow's nest atop Flotsam already behind us, and the thick trees along the marshy, lower reaches of Hampsfield Fell some distance ahead. I was cold, soaked with seawater, and blessedly thankful—even more thankful when the shoreline finally hove toward us in a rush. The wagon was thrown onto the beach by the tide, wheels forward, and we rolled across twenty feet of sandy shingle in a mad instant and straight on into the marsh, where we quickly lost momentum, slowing to a stop in a pool of dark water that sat amid the trees. The diving chamber with its prize inside was still miraculously secured to the crane, and it swung back and forth slowly like the pendulum of an enormous clock. ⟿

Chapter 8

Smothercated

THE MORNING WAS PEACEFULLY silent but for the calling of gulls, the cool spring sun filtered through the leaves of the tree limbs overhead, and Morecambe Bay lay as placid as a lake behind us, the tidewaters a thing of memory. It was as if we had stepped out of the tumult of a noisy ball into the silent peace of a garden.

"Stay well clear of the pool," I said, looking down at the swampy ground beneath us. The wagon settled more deeply into the mire even as we watched, as if the sands of the Bay and its marshy environs were determined to consume us. Finn leapt clear, landing on his feet, and I followed, coming down on solid ground with an ankle-numbing force.

"Look, sir! She's in a hurry now!" Finn said, pointing at the forward part of the wagon, which slipped a couple of inches deeper again, the pool emitting a soft, deadly, well-fed sigh. The canted-down, forward deck of the wagon was buried, sandy mud oozing up over the bench, the diving chamber leaning away from the crane mast.

"If we make the grappling hook and line fast around a tree," I said, "we might still haul the wagon out with the block and tackle and save the diving chamber and the box."

"I'll try for the hook," Finn said gamely, and he paced backwards several yards and set out as if to make a rash leap onto the bed. I stopped him in mid-stride. Leaping down from a height was one thing, but leaping upward entirely another.

"Perhaps a tree limb," I said, and we looked above us now. Our luck held fair, for some ten feet overhead a leafy limb reached out over the wagon.

"Give me a heft, sir," Finn said, and in an instant he was up and standing on my shoulders. He leapt, caught a lower limb, and scampered into the tree like a forest creature. I stepped back to watch him. Getting a line on the wagon would be easy enough, if we were quick about it, although hauling it out again might want the team of horses, if in fact it could be hauled out.

There was abruptly the sound of voices from some-where very near, and in my current state of mind I thought that it was St. Ives, come to fetch us. But then I knew that it wasn't his voice, and I turned to see two men appearing from along a trail that followed the edge of the Bay—the two men I had first seen in Lambert Court, playing the part of workmen. The tall one carried his rifle; the short, simian-looking man who had struck Merton had only his ugly countenance to recommend him. They seemed as astonished to see me as I was to see them, but it was only in that regard that we were equal, for there were two of them and one of me, and there was the rifle to consider. A smile flickered across the face of the tall man, if indeed you could call it a smile, as he glanced from me to the wagon. He slowly raised the rifle and pointed it at me. I assumed that he meant to shoot me, and so I stood perfectly still, hoping that Finn was doing the same in the tree.

"What have we here, Spanker?" the tall man said.

"A hideous devil, I do believe," Spanker said. "Pity its poor mother."

"I say that if it moves it's a corpse, but if it stays still it might be of some small value to men like us."

"It's brought us the undersea chamber," the man Spanker said. "Isn't it a good 'un, returning the doctor's stolen property?"

"A peach. Sit down and have a rest, mate," the tall one said to me, "there by that tree. Spanker, twist his head for him if he gets fancy. I'll find a piece of rope to secure that wagon, and then we'll see what his friends think he's worth—a couple of quid and the odd pence, I should think."

I sat down as requested, not anxious to have my head twisted, and watched the tall man head off through the close trees. A horse whinnied in that direction, and I saw that a canvas tent and bits and pieces of gear stood some distance beyond our clearing, lost in the woods unless you knew where to look. A sort of dogcart or shay was tethered nearby them. It was a neatly hidden bivouac, close enough to the road so that they must have seen and heard us early this morning when we were rattling along toward Grange-over-Sands in our wagon. Frosticos, of course, had posted them there. How they communicated with the doctor, I couldn't say, but I recalled what St. Ives had speculated about underground waters and passages inland, and it would seem no great feat for Frosticos to surface now and then a mile or so north in the lower reaches of the River Kent, where it broadened out and entered the Bay.

I stole a casual glance into the treetops, and spotted Finn straight off, perched over the wagon among the leaves. He was anxious to be up to something, and was gesturing furiously. He pointed at me, put his hands together as if praying, and pretended to dive headfirst from his limb. I had no idea what he meant, but then he repeated the gesture, pointing determinedly at me again, and I understood: he wanted *me* to do the plunging. Apparently he had gone mad.

The tall man had by now reached the clearing in the woods, and would doubtless soon return. Spanker was paring his fingernails with a murderous-looking knife. He gave me a malicious grin, and I grinned back, the seconds passing quickly. *Trust the boy*, my misgiving mind told me, and before it could tell me anything different, I leapt forward from where I sat and threw myself bodily into the quicksand, trying to scoop my way to the wagon, but bogging down almost at once, too far from solid ground, however, to be easily retrieved.

Spanker stared at me with a look of surprised wonder on his face, but that changed to something else again when he saw Finn drop out of the tree and onto the bed of the wagon, at which moment he began to shout incoherently for his companion. I held very still, feeling myself sinking, fighting the urge to kick my feet and fully expecting to be shot. Within seconds Finn had slipped the catch on the windlass and was hauling out line, swinging the grappling hook and letting it fly out toward me over a distance of perhaps ten feet. I latched onto it, and straightaway I heard the windlass turning and began towing forward across the surface of the muck. I looked back, and saw that the tall man had returned, and that he held a coil of rope. His rifle, however, stood against the tree, and the smile still twisted his mouth.

We had no place to go. He saw that. We were making good our escape, but onto a variety of sinking ship. I reached the wagon and hefted myself over the side, the quicksand holding the wagon steady in its grip, although it was apparently sliding downward at a steeper and steeper angle, the diving chamber swinging out farther on its tether, dangling a mere foot above the surface now. In a moment it would simply be out of reach.

"The chamber," I said to Finn in a low voice, and he caught my meaning directly. Without a pause I reached far out and managed to open the hatch, drawing the chamber closer to us. I shoveled Finn through the door, and than climbed in myself, throwing out the broken remains of the strongbox before locking us in. I picked up the odd, ovoid device that Parson Grimstead had recovered from his manure pile and set it carefully on the seat. It was the size of a large loaf of bread, built of several riveted metals, brass and copper among them. Despite its having remained dry in the rubber-sealed strongbox, the brass and copper were discolored with faint lines of verdigris. One of the ends was contrived of a crystalline substance, separated from the metals by a band of ebony-like wood. The crystal was translucent, but was cloudy with striations, so that it obscured whatever lay beneath it.

"May I take a squint at it, sir?" Finn asked, and I could see no reason to deny him. We certainly had nothing better to do with our time. He picked it up, holding it by the ends and peering into the crystal. Right then the wagon gave another downward jolt. There was the sound of laughter from our two friends on shore, and the tall one waved at us in a cheerful, bon voyage sort of way. Then they set about getting a line out to us.

"It's warm-like," Finn said. "Like an egg under a hen. I wonder what it does."

It did feel curiously warm, although it hadn't a moment ago, and either the sun was shining on it so as to make the crystal glow faintly, or else it was glowing of its own accord. Certainly we had done nothing to it aside from picking it up. It was decidedly close in the chamber, and so I turned the valve to let in air, and there was a satisfying blast, although nothing like its original pressure. Soon we would have to do something decisive or else give ourselves up. Either way, it was better to do so before the chamber sank into the sands than after.

And with that thought I had a look at the controls of the chamber, wishing I had paid more attention earlier.

Still and all, St. Ives had figured them out, and I supposed I could do the same to some useful extent. Straight off I found the lever that emptied the ballast tanks, and I resolutely drained them, giving our friends on shore a moment of pause. We would at least ride higher in the quicksand, I thought.

Then another thought came to me: if the line affixing the chamber to the windlass were released, we might still float. Even if the wagon sank to the very bottom of the swamp, it wouldn't drag us down with it. What had St. Ives said?—two hundred feet of line? As I saw it, the wagon was our anchor....

"I'm going to open the hatch," I said. "Can you pop out and release the stop on the windlass line so that the chamber might float?"

"Done," Finn said, laying the device on the seat. I threw the hatch open and in a trice he was out and had released the line. I was surprised by the sudden plummet of the craft—a plummet of perhaps six inches—onto the surface of the pool. Finn clambered back into the chamber and shut the door behind him, picking up the device and holding it again, as if he meant to keep it safe. I immediately doubted myself, full of the unsettling notion that we were sinking deeper into the ooze now, that the broad expanse of the wagon had in fact been our temporary security.

On shore, the tall man gave us a discerning look, but again seemed to find our activities irrelevant, as perhaps they were. They had their own line run out and around the trunk of the tree now, and Spanker, who had the build of a Navy topman, was quickly aloft. Within moments he dropped heavily to the deck, ignoring us utterly until he had secured the line to the base of the crane mast. Then he pitched the grappling hook shoreward, and the tall man gave it a turn about the tree, and Spanker moved across to the windlass, where he took the slack out of the rope. He made an effort to turn it farther, to winch the wagon up out of the quicksand, but to little avail. They had a double line on it now, though. No doubt to their mind, the chamber was safe enough. Spanker stepped across the deck toward us. He bent down and made a series of loathsome faces before silently acting out the antics of a man in the throes of suffocation, after which he shook his head sadly, winked at us, and disappeared back up into the tree.

"We're in the hopper," Finn said, "and no doubt about it. But my money's on the Professor and old Mr. Merton. They'll be along directly."

"Surely they will," I said.

"Look at this, sir." Finn said, nodding at the device now. The crystal had a more pronounced glow, from deep within, and it was blood-warm to the touch. "I believe it's woke up," Finn said. "What does it do, do you suppose?"

The term *woke up* alarmed me. "*Do?*" I asked. "I'm afraid I can't say. Professor St. Ives seems to believe that it was connected with the odd behavior of cattle, but that tells us little."

"Cattle, is it?" He gave me a skeptical look.

There was a decisive sucking noise now, directly below us, and the chamber shuddered and shifted. We held very still. I was certain now that releasing the line had murdered us, that we were sinking, and that someone—Frosticos or St. Ives—would fish the chamber out of the quicksand with two corpses inside.

But we didn't sink. We shifted and shuddered and sat still again. Then we shuddered, as if the wind were blowing, and kept on shuddering. The two on shore were eating a jolly breakfast now, with a pot of tea and two cups—all very elegant, and meant, no doubt, simply to torment us. Spanker held up a great chunk of bread and jam, raised it in a greedy salute, and devoured it. But the tall one noticed the antics of the chamber, and he set down his teacup and gave us a hard look, as if we were up to something.

And apparently we were, quite literally, for instead of sinking, we seemed to be rising. "We're off," Finn said, matter-of-factly. "It's the device, sure as you're born. Same as one of those hot air balloons, maybe."

That made no sense at all to me. How could it be *the device*? Hot air balloons? We had seemed to become one. We rose slowly, looking slightly downward onto the two on shore now. The tall man shouted something to Spanker, who climbed hurriedly into the tree, moving out onto his limb just after we had drifted past it. He glanced up at us, and he wasn't grimacing and gesturing now, but was apparently mystified and suspicious. He stepped straight off the limb and latched onto the rope, which had begun to unreel itself like a charmed serpent. The chamber rocked with his weight, and for a moment was actually descending, putting an end to our capers. Our descent quickly slowed, and for a moment we rocked lazily in stasis. And then once again we were off, as Finn had put it, with Spanker still dangling tenaciously below us, kicking and tugging.

"He's off his chump," Finn said. "Why did he go for the rope when there's a winch in easy reach?"

"He doesn't have much of a chump to start with," I said.

The craft swung and shook as Spanker struggled futilely to accomplish what gravity had failed to accomplish. And then, perhaps realizing that he was dangerously high above the deck of the wagon and that we were drifting to leeward despite the sea anchor, he let go, heaving himself toward the deck of the wagon below, the chamber canting sideways with the force of it. We looked down in time to see him turn in the air, head downward and still a couple of narrow feet from the wagon when he smashed head-foremost into the quicksand with enough force to bury him waist deep, one arm trapped by his side and his legs waving, as in that painting of the fall of Icarus. His free arm and legs worked furiously, driving him downward. The tall man tore at the knotted rope (which, fittingly, Spanker had himself knotted) but he was taking far too long about it. The wind drifted us north, so that we got a better view of the scene below, and what we saw was the tall man pointlessly casting the rope at his erstwhile companion's ankles in the moment that he slipped beneath the sands and disappeared.

It was in fact a ghastly sight, despite Spanker's criminal tendencies, and the odd notion came into my mind that I wished I hadn't known the man's name. Perhaps it's not odd. I tried to think of something sufficiently philosophical to say to Finn, but the boy was already nodding his head in contemplation. "In Duffy's Circus," he told me, "old Samson the elephant sat down on his trainer, something like a tea cosy over the teapot, if you see what I mean. He was a terrible man named Walsh, and his head went straight up the hiatus. The doctor told us that Samson smothercated him dead."

I wondered in that moment, from my elevated perspective, how I had ever come to doubt the boy. My doubts had all been speculative. His actions had clearly professed his innocence and loyalty. A high regard for one's powers of logic, I told myself, can smothercate a man.

"Take a look down the way, sir," Finn said now, pointing out toward the Bay.

I took a look. It was St. Ives and Fred Merton, perhaps a quarter mile down toward Grange-over-Sands, coming along the trail by the shore. Merton carried a rifle. They had seen us right enough, floating there high above the treetops, and they stood for a moment marveling at the sight. As for us, we could see far out into the broad Atlantic, the dark line westward being the shore of Ireland, I believe, and the Isle of Man sitting in the sea in between. I opened the hatch, leaning out into the giddy breeze, and pointed downward, toward where the tall man stood at the edge of the pool in dazed contemplation. He apparently saw the signal himself, deduced that reinforcements had arrived, and set out at a dead run toward his camp, carrying his rifle.

St. Ives and Merton were wary, of course, and came along much more slowly. By the time they reached the camp our assailant had fled in his shay, leaving his accoutrements behind. From our height we could see him scouring along the road in the distance, but there was nothing at all to do about it, which was a dirty shame. Hasbro had been shot twice in the space of a few days by the same man, a man who had no motive aside from mere sport, which says something about human degradation that I'd rather not soil these pages speculating upon. Justice, I'm afraid, sometimes is not met out on Earth, or at least not that we know of. But then I'm reminded of Spanker, burrowing his way to Hell, and I find that there's little satisfaction in that sort of justice anyway.

We descended from our height after a good deal of shouted communication with St. Ives. The device—an anti-gravity mechanism that reacted quite simply to heat—bodily heat and radiant sunlight in our case—gradually lost its powers when Finn was induced simply to set it down onto the deck of the chamber. Later St. Ives speculated that the naturally high degree of heat in the manure heap on Parson Grimstead's property had been sufficient to elevate the immediately surrounding cattle. Our descent was every bit as graceful as our ascent, although far more disappointing, for I rather enjoyed the view.

As for Dr. Frosticos, he and his submarine didn't reappear, and so we had no choice but to keep his diving chamber until he called for it. We took a certain joy in the fact that he had failed in all his endeavors, and that in his last, mad rush in the submarine he had passed out of our lives again, at least for a time. —

Uncle Wiggily,

an Afterword to "The Ebb Tide"
By James P. Blaylock

The Muse on a Volkswagen Bus

A S SOME FEW OF my readers know (perhaps very few) the first of my stories involving Professor Langdon St. Ives appeared in *UNEARTH* magazine in 1977. It was titled "The Ape-box Affair," and along with St. Ives it introduced the young Jack Owlesby, who in fact is a character in the story as well as the "I" who narrates it. (Although it's often not revealed in the texts, Owlesby narrates all of the St. Ives stories, sometimes writing in the first person, sometimes in the third as the whim strikes him. Owlesby seems to want to be a writer as well as an historian.) It also introduced Dorothy Keeble, Jack's future wife (named "Olivia" in the "Ape-box Affair" as a courtesy to the young woman: the events of the story are very recent at the time of the narration, and Owlesby would have avoided taking the liberty of using her actual name, although he doesn't scruple against using the actual names of the other, older characters. One of the avowed purposes of his work is to promote and chronicle the adventures of Langdon St. Ives.) The plot of "The Ape-box Affair" hinges on a confusion of several mechanized boxes built by William Keeble, toy maker extraordinaire. Some of the incidents, characters, and trappings of "The Ape-box Affair" found their way into the first St. Ives novel, *Homunculus*, published several years later. Some of them did not—the picking and choosing having occurred, I'll insist, in the interest of what might be called "truth," which, like Uncle Wiggily's infamous bar of laundry soap, is a slippery eel at best.

I had published only one real story previous to "The Ape-box Affair," also in *UNEARTH*, a very different sort of piece involving an imaginative boy riding aboard a Greyhound bus that might or might not be bound for Mars, which he might or might not have confused with a red agate marble in his pants pocket. In the further interest of truth, such as it is, I'll insist now that the boy in that story was me, although I didn't know it at the time that I wrote it; certainly it was my agate marble that he had in his pocket, and his state of imaginative confusion was very like my own in those days.The story was generated by an incident that's still fresh in my mind, although it occurred more than 35 years ago. A bunch of us—Tim Powers, Bill Bailey (later to marry Tim's sister Beth) my wife Viki, and I were driving into L.A. in our friend Neil's Volkswagen bus, bound for Canter's Delicatessen. The usual wild conversation ensued nonstop, and someone put a question to me. I didn't respond, my mind being elsewhere, as it so often is. After a silent moment Neil said, "Blaylock thinks he's riding on a Greyhound bus to Mars." Everyone laughed, including me, although I was already thinking about the story the comment suggested. In those days I carried several good luck charms in my pocket, including the agate marble that figures into that story. I sometimes still seem to be aboard that Greyhound bus—a long, strange trip....

The Muse in an Airship

"Uncle Wiggily went to a store where they sold toy circus balloons, and of the monkey gentleman who kept the store he asked:

'Have you any flying machines?'

'What do you mean—flying machines?' asked the monkey gentleman. 'Do you mean birds?'

'Well, birds are flying machines, of course,' the rabbit gentleman said. 'But I mean a sort of

airship that I could go up in as if I were in a
balloon, and fly around in the clouds...."

When I was growing up my family occasionally
played the Uncle Wiggily board game, in which one was
pursued through the swamp by the bad Pipsisewah and
the terrible Skeezicks. I loved the game, even though it
gave me nightmares. Later on I discovered the Uncle
Wiggily books, written by Howard R. Garis, and I'm still
particularly fond of Uncle Wiggily's Airship, in which
Uncle Wiggily builds his airship by tying balloons to a
laundry basket. He fastens an electric fan to it for pro-
pulsion and contrives a sort of hockey-stick tiller and
"a baby carriage wheel to steer by," and then embarks on
a series of high altitude adventures, often suffering crash
landings when the balloons burst. In one adventure he's
saved by the ingenuity of Arabella the chicken girl, who
blows flotational soap bubbles through a pipe: "Then she
blew forty-'leven bubbles, or maybe more, for all I know.
Uncle Wiggily caught them, and fastened them with silk
threads and cobwebs, which a kind spider lady spun for
him, to the basket of his airship...."

Back in the early 1980s a man in Long Beach fastened
helium balloons to a lawn chair and floated high over
the city, eating a sack lunch and rising to heights above
10,000 feet, where he was viewed with astonishment by

pilots and passengers of commercial airplanes. When he landed, hours later, sunburned and amazed, he was cited by the FAA for having failed to file a flight plan. There were no other relevant laws on the books, apparently, although there are now. We're living in an era when Uncle Wiggily would be an outlaw, and the monkey gentleman and Arabella the chicken girl accessories to a crime. (Uncle Wiggily, by the way, took a Japanese umbrella up with him to solve the sunburn problem.) We hear often enough that truth is stranger than fiction, which is obviously true if you keep your eyes open. It's wonderful, however, when reality mimics fiction, and an unemployed car mechanic out in Long Beach goes down to a store where they sell toy circus balloons and becomes Uncle Wiggily for a day.

I remember reading the account of the balloon airship in the newspaper—reading it more than once—and then driving down to the Lucky supermarket on Chapman Avenue in a highly distracted state of mind. I bounced up over the curb on my way into the parking lot (my mind elsewhere) the jolt coincidental with the inspiration for the first chapter of what would become *The Digging Leviathan*. Later that afternoon I actually started writing the novel (which Lester del Rey would later reject unread, on the grounds that the idea of the book was "cultistic." "You went to the same damned university that Powers

went to, didn't you?" Lester asked me over the telephone.)
The episode of the balloon airship disappeared out of the
book in the writing of it; it had simply been a sort of
incidental muse.

The Muse in a Steamer Trunk

When those first two *UNEARTH* stories were published, neither generated wild interest, but more than
one reader commented on the odd differences in style
and method, as if the stories had been written by different authors. I mean to address that phenomenon briefly,
because those perceptive readers were to some small
degree correct, and these thirty years later, after writing
and publishing some sixteen novels and enough short
stories to have lost count, I see no reason that the truth
shouldn't prevail, such as it is.

In 1975, Viki and I traveled to Europe for a period of
nearly three months, spending some time in England and
Ireland. We stayed briefly in Bristol with our friends Sue
and Barry Watts. Barry had developed carpentry skills
building wooden boats, and had recently contracted to
do some restoration work at St. Mary Redcliffe Church.
His project was to restore the large, wood-and-stone
garden shed in back of the Sexton's house next door. The
shed was a comparatively recent addition to the grounds
of the medieval church, having been built early in the

1920s. In World War II a German bomb blew apart a tramway nearby, the blast throwing a tram rail through the roof. (The errant rail is now a memorial on the church grounds.) The shed had been ineptly repaired, and time and the weather had been nearly as disastrous as the tram rail in the years since. Restoring the shed would take Barry a couple of months of finely detailed work. The details of that work, as interesting as they were, are irrelevant to this account, aside from my helping with the early business of removing the contents of the shed to a nearby garage. Over the years the shed had been used as a sort of warehouse, and it was packed with otherwise homeless junk. It reminded me a little of a yard sale, in that there was nothing apparently interesting about any of it except for the lurking possibility of some small, hidden treasure....

In the end, I had more fun puttering around in that old garden shed during the three days we were in Bristol than I had looking at all the cathedrals and museums and "sites" that Europe afforded us during the rest of our long holiday, and on top of that, I found my hidden treasure, such as it turned out to be. Statutes of limitation and copyright being what they are, there's no danger in my admitting that now. There were a number of wooden crates with screwed-down lids piled against the back wall, and of course it was none of our business to look inside, although we wanted to badly. There was a steamer trunk, however, out of keeping with the rest of the crates and buried beneath them, which no one had gone to the trouble to lock. I simply couldn't help myself; I took a look inside. I was disappointed at first to find nothing much in it—some personal documents and vaguely interesting old magazines (more interesting when I came to understand what they were). At the bottom of the trunk, however, lay a number of parcels wrapped in calfskin and tied neatly—manuscripts of some sort, apparently (or allegedly) written down nearly a century earlier. I had no idea by whom until later, when I had the leisure to study them.

But I'm getting ahead of myself. What happened was that I left Barry to his work and read through some of it on the spot, quickly coming to a decision that—I'm ashamed to say—could be viewed as reprehensible, not least of all because I took advantage of a friend. That afternoon I boxed up the manuscripts and mailed them home. I wasn't guilty of theft, mind you, because as soon as I had the opportunity I photocopied all of them and then mailed the originals back to Bristol, where Barry was just then finishing his work. He returned them to their trunk, put the trunk back into the pile of crates and junk, and several days later moved out to Harrogate where he opened a fish and chips restaurant.

"The Ape-box Affair" was (substantially) one of those manuscripts—and so my guilt perpetuated itself when I mailed it to *UNEARTH* as my own work, although the story originated with Jack Owlesby. I'll insist, however, that his was unpublishable as it stood. Parts of it were fragmentary, for one thing: the first half was mainly a collection of notes and odd paragraphs. The alchemy that turned it into a story was of my own devising. I considered sending it out as the work of Jack Owlesby, but it seemed to me that UNEARTH, having published one story by Blaylock, might be induced to publish another, whereas they wouldn't have heard of Jack Owlesby, and wouldn't be able to contact the man in any event. You can imagine that I wasn't keen on the idea of explaining how the manuscript had fallen into my hands. The editors wouldn't have touched it. It turned out to be monumentally simple to rationalize the entire business, and to incorporate Jack Owlesby into myself, so to speak: Owlesby was a mere ghost, after all (and so didn't need the forty dollars, money being of no value in the afterlife).

It's sufficient to point out that Jack Owlesby didn't live to publish his own manuscripts, or to explain or eradicate their inconsistencies and put them into order. You might suppose that I myself would have eradicated inconsistencies, both of style and content, but that would have required reading and reworking the entirety of those bundled manuscripts—essentially rewriting all of it—back in 1976. I didn't have the patience for it then, and I don't have the patience for it now, except in my piecemeal fashion. All in the fullness of time, I say, and to hell with the flight plan.

And so the voice, literarily speaking, of the "The Ape-box Affair" is to some small extent my own, as is the voice of *The Ebb Tide*, although I'm certainly not the "I" of either story, as has already been revealed. It's best, I suppose, to say that the voice is collaborative (which tells us nothing, since voice in that sense is always collaborative: it can't exist without character, and character can't exist without an author. Huck Finn's "voice" isn't Twain's exactly; but is a collaboration between the living author and the imagined character). Plenty of authors have insisted that their characters "write" their stories, and that they—the authors—simply follow along, and I suppose that's more or less true; it's simply a little more true in the case of the St. Ives stories.

Ultimately, to what extent the stories of Langdon St. Ives are my own, and to what extent they're the work of Jack Owlesby, is neither here nor there. Haggling over the issue is pointless. The copyrights are mine. I'll insist that if I hadn't borrowed the manuscripts, and if I hadn't rewritten them and finished them and published them as my own, Langdon St. Ives and his many adventures would still lie buried in the darkness of that steamer trunk, in much the same sense that unwritten stories lie buried in the writer's mind. Jack Owlesby would remain a mere ghost, living in a garden shed in Bristol. In the end, that intrepid car mechanic in Long Beach, whether he knew it or not, owed a debt to Uncle Wiggily, who perfected the science of balloon airship navigation seventy years earlier, and who never bothered to file a flight plan, either.

—◦◦◦—

It's my belief that "The Ape-box Affair" was undertaken as a work of fiction, with certain recent incidents in the life of Langdon St. Ives being the inspiration. It's apparently the work of a young writer. *The Ebb Tide*, however, which occurs at the time of the Phoenix Park murders (and so we can set the date absolutely—May 6, 1822, some seven years after the events chronicled in Homunculus) is something more like a history or a memoir. Owlesby is older now, not half so giddy. There are fewer apparent fabulations and shaggy-doggisms, and Owlesby has developed some admirable self-doubt and a penchant for philosophizing. That's due, I'll insist, to the increasing sobriety of age, and it's altogether fitting that I was a young writer myself when I undertook to put "The Ape-box Affair" into publishable shape.

One interesting thing: there's no indication anywhere concerning when, exactly, the stories were in fact written. I've merely been speculating. Owlesby might have written "The Ape-box Affair" in later years, perhaps when he was doddering into a second childhood, or—equally possibly— after he had taken to drink. I speculated when I first read the manuscript (speaking again of muses) that Owlesby had been heavily influenced by Stevenson, in particular by *The Dynamiter* and the stories in *The New Arabian Nights*, although when I checked copyright dates I discovered that those books weren't published until the mid 1880s, and the events of "The Ape-box Affair" must have occurred prior to 1875, a decade earlier. All of my speculations, in other words, might be nonsense. Questions of origin are further muddled by the fact that in the original texts there are very few clues to reveal when the various events actually took place.

Truth (that slippery eel) exists, but time and tide have hidden it from us, and there's no way to get at it now. If we're to keep afloat, we're left to balloons and an electric fan, and to the bubbles and cobweb of the imagination. ⁓

—Jim Blaylock